PROCULA

Marion H. Youngquist

GARY DRURY PUBLISHER | KENTUCKY

Anniversary Edition

ISBN-13: 978-0692747391 (Gary Drury Publishing)
ISBN-10: 0692747397

Library of Congress Control Number: 2005924709

ISBN-13: 978-0-9770533-1-5
ISBN-10: 0-9770533-1-8
ISBN-13: 978-0-9770533-0-8 (CD ROM eBook)
ISBN-10: 0-9770533-0-X (CD ROM eBook)

www.druryspublishing.com

KENTUCKY

Printed in the United States of America.

for Ted, teacher, pastor, husband

PREFACE

Since childhood, I've been intrigued by the singular Bible verse in Matthew's gospel which mentions Pilate's wife. With a twinkle in her eyes, my mother said, "Pilate should have listened to his wife. He would have saved himself a lot of trouble!"

Several novels have been written about Pilate, but few – that I could find – about his wife. Through the years, I pursued other stories, but postponed writing about Procula (so named from apocryphal sources).

On September 11, 2001 my life – like many – changed because of the Twin Towers disaster. Two days later, my husband Ted and I were in New York City, staying near Union Square where poignant vigils and stark memorials mourned the victims. Acrid ash hung heavy in the air. Picture flyers of missing persons haunted us. We realized that many people would never fulfill their dreams.

That weekend, we sailed to Bermuda – a somber cruise. From the ship's library, I read Desire of the Everlasting Hills by Thomas Cahill, a historian's view of Jesus. When I returned home, I read a fine historical study of Pontius Pilate by Ann Wroe, a London author and editor. These two books rekindled my desire to write about Pilate's wife. I still had time to fulfill my dream. I began her story.

The interest of family and friends encouraged me. Valuable critiques were made by: Mary Mulroy, Director of the Wauwatosa, Wisconsin Public Library; Dr Tim Crain, Professor of History, University of Wisconsin – Milwaukee; and Dr. Lucille Rosenberg, a Milwaukee child psychiatrist (retired) and poet.

Manuscript help came from Grace Gunnlaugsson and Knute Jacobson. Readers included Sue and Bill Romo, LaVerne Wuebben and her son Robert, Becky Ramirez, Dorothea Winek, Sue Jacobson, Eleanor "Ellie" Ellison, Mary Smith, Dr. Karl Barth, Ted and our children – Eric and wife Barbara, Marcia and Ed (Hunter), Margaret and Steve (Fleming), Mary Ellen (Karalis), and our Mexican daughter, Alma Vera. Technical assistance was provided by Susan Klopfer and Justin Kutka. I'm very grateful that Gary Drury Publishing, Hodgenville, KY wanted to see my manuscript.

When we lived in Glen Ellyn, IL, my dear friend Sara Hill (now deceased) critiqued my stories when I began writing fiction. My pursuit and fulfillment stems from her many hours of encouragement.

To all I can only say Thank you, Thank you, Thank you.

Marion Neal Horn Youngquist
Wauwatosa, Wisconsin

TIME LINE

EASTERN TERRITORY--Rulers and Divisions

6 B.C.E. - Birth of Christ

37 B.C. E. - 4 B.C.E. Herod the Great rules

At his death, the Eastern Territory was divided
between three sons:

4 B.C.E. - 34 C.E. Philip, the Tetrarch
(Batanea-northeastern area, 1/4)

4 B.C.E. - 39 C.E. Herod Antipas, the Tetrarch
(Galilee-north and Peraea, east.1/4th)

4 B.C.E. - 6 C.E. Herod Archaelaus, the Ethnarch
(Judaea, Samaritis, Idumaea, 1/2)

6 C.E. Province of Judaea, Samaritis and
Idumaea established.

Prefects:

Coponius 6 C.E. - 9 C.E.
Ambivius 9 C.E. - 12 C.E.
Annius Rufus 12 C.E. - 15 C.E.

14 C.E. Emperor Augustus dies
Emperor Tiberius (Augustus'
stepson) rules

Prefects:

Valerius Gratus 15 C.E. - 26 C.E.
Pontius Pilate 26 C.E. - 36 C.E.

29 C.E. John the Baptist is beheaded in Peraea.

33 C.E. Jesus of Nazareth is crucified in Judaea.

36   C.E. Pontius Pilate is recalled to Roma.

37   C.E. Emperor Tiberius dies

ROMAN EMPIRE - PRINCIPATES

27 B.C.E. - 14 C.E. Gaius Julius Caesar Octavianus
(Augustus)
14 C.E. - 37 C.E. Tiberius Claudius Nero Caesar
37 C.E. - 41 C.E. Gaius Caesar Germanicus
(Caligula)

PROCULA occurs primarily during the reign of Tiberius.

. . . Besides, while Pilate was sitting on the judgement seat, his wife sent word to him, have nothing to do with that righteous man, for I have suffered much over him today in a dream.

Matthew 27:19

This novel is fiction based on historical personalities and events.

An asterisk indicates further explanation under Notes.

Chapter I

hen Pilate, Tuum and I sailed from Caesarea last week, I hoped my nightmares were left behind. Not so. Even here in Alexandria within the safe walls of Lucius' compound, one of my most disturbing dreams haunted me again last night.

Noise – the noise is incredible. Then I remember my father's house in far-off Arretium where we sat at the table in midsummer, sipping sweet wine and eating olives, goat cheese and crusty bread. How I long for a summer like that. Instead, I'm here in a banquet hall with the guests half-drunk, tossing bread sticks in mock fights and weaving unsteadily across the room. My husband will come later and make a grand entrance with his entourage – an entrance that will impress everyone with his prestige and position as Prefect of Judaea. To think that I've ended up here, beyond the Great Sea.

*Antipas, the Tetrarch, (who would like to call himself King) is bleary-eyed and paunchy. His speech is garbled. He claps his hands.

"Shplay!" he signals the musicians. The drummer taps a rhythmic beat as a flute and lyre join in harmony.

From a side room, his step-daughter *Salome enters, swaying to the music. She is pudgy. Perhaps she has seen thirteen summers. Swathed in filmy red silk, she begins to dance – if that is what you call it. She is not graceful, but woodenly goes through the motions. She raises a hand above her head, making jerky circles while she twirls awkwardly.

I watch her mother *Herodias who was once married to the Tetrarch's brother. The woman has a sly smile on her face. She moves her shoulders, nods her head as if signaling young Salome to dance more seductively. I find the girl's performance more sad than suggestive. I slip away, out onto a cool marble balcony. I feel so alone. I am glad to be away from the raucous laughter and poor entertainment.

I came to the party as a good-will gesture. My husband, *Pilate, will join me later. He doesn't trust the Tetrarch and avoids eating at his table. But I, a loyal wife and of less importance, can toy with my food and chance the wine. Dare I ask — would it matter if I died? A wife is easily replaced. Perhaps Antipas would offer his clumsy stepdaughter to remain in Roma's favor.

The music stops. I must return to my place. As I slip into the room, I find the mood of the party has suddenly shifted. Something has happened. I hesitate to speak to people, lest I give some oblique signal or favor to a particular group. Roma rules because it stands above the petty factions that vie for power here, so I wait for Pilate to come striding in with a confident air, superior to Antipas and his fiefdom.

Guests are whispering. I can't understand this dialect very well. I depend on dear Tuum, my maid who never went to school as I did but speaks a half-dozen languages. She leaves to refill my wine glass. The evening wears on. Finally, the servants come in with plates of stuffed dates, honeyed pastries, spicy nuts and sweet grapes. I eat a handful — watching, waiting for whatever will happen.

Trumpet notes announce a grand entrance. I expect to see Pilate enter with his royal guard. I half-rise to meet him. Instead, a servant hobbles in bearing the bloodied head of some prisoner on a silver platter — wild eyes staring into this final death-trap.

I scream.

I awaken with Tuum shaking me. "Bibi! Bibi! Wake up! It's the bad dream again."

Although she is a bit younger than I, she holds me against her breast like a loving mother. In a few moments, I grow quiet, accustom my eyes to the darkness that lingers just before dawn.

"Oh, Tuum, you are so good to me."

"You are the one who is good. You rescued me."

I smile with a memory better than the dream. Once, Tuum — so dear to me — was owned by a rug merchant in Roma. I, also, know what it is to be indebted to another. When I recall my story, I understand why Tuum and

16

PROCULA | Marion H. Youngquist

I have such a close relationship. We have been together for over twenty years.

Tuum pads over the cool stone floor. She pours a goblet of water. I take small sips. She wipes my brow with a damp towel. I close my eyes with a deep sigh. I will feign sleep, so Tuum can get her rest. These early hours will be spent mulling over my life – how I happen to be here and what the future may bring when we leave tomorrow. Then I will pray to *Yahveh – the One who can be trusted – and sleep.

For almost a decade, I've been troubled by that ghastly experience. Sometimes another bloodied face also haunts my dreams. Often, I relive both experiences. However, I wasn't the only one affected that night. Women fainted. Men rushed from the room, covering their mouths, only to hang retching over a marble balustrade. The guests quickly dispersed as Antipas stumbled away, steadied by two servants. Even Herodias, head haughtily held high, left the room pale and shaken.

When our group left *Machaerus, I vowed never to be in Herod Antipas' presence again. Then I wished to be back in Roma! We had soothsayers and holy men there, but we didn't kill them. We let them shake their fists and utter dire warnings in the name of Apollo or Diabolus. We Romans had various kinds of gods. We borrowed many from the Greeks. Zeus became our Jupiter and Ares was changed to our Mars. This multiplicity of gods amused Pilate. He scorned them all.

"The gods claim Absolute Truth. . . or so their faithful followers believe. I bow to all and none!" he laughed. "I only believe in Roma's power. Hail to the Emperor!"

However, when Pilate took his eastern post, he discovered the Judaeans believed differently. Truth only came from their deity, Yahveh, who claimed them as a chosen people through his divine will. Yahveh was an unseen yet living god. No statue existed of him. A person could not bargain with Yahveh like we Romans did with our gods. This mysterious deity demanded their devotion yet cared for his people. If I were a Judaean, would Yahveh erase that awful night at Machaerus from my memory? Or was I always doomed to live with that bloody scene? I pondered about that evening for a long time.   Dreams often haunted me. Maybe my mother's death caused them. As a child, I struggled with curious dreams. Always, there was a barrier. I would discover a heavy wooden door that wouldn't open, although I fiercely pounded on it. Only once, I pushed it open and went into blinding light. When I looked back, the door was still there – shut tight. I pounded to get back outside again. I woke up, flailing the air with my fists.

In another dream I carefully crossed a river, bridged by a heavy log. When I reached the center – over the rushing current – the log began to roll. I danced little steps to keep my balance. I felt myself falling into the cold water.

If I told Cook about my dreams, she'd say that I had too many sweets after my supper. Next day she'd feed me a nourishing vegetable soup to restore my health. She thought her thick peasant mixture cured everything. That was many years ago. When I still have vivid nightmares, I secretly wish for a bowl of that wonderful soup to restore my health. It remains a pleasant memory of Arretium, my birthplace.

In Caesarea, Tuum calmed my fears. When Pilate was away or working late, Tuum would suggest that we climb to the palace rooftop. We watched many colorful sunsets streak the evening sky with pale peach and aqua tints. We played board games, or I practiced my flute (playing rather badly). Tuum always clapped her hands for more. She was my slave and knew how slaves gained approval from their owners.

I encouraged Tuum to draw pictures, which she did quite well – intricate stylized flowers and birds, reminiscent of rug patterns in her former master's shop. When we grew quiet, I looked at the first evening star and thought about my life. How did I end up in Judaea, so far from Italia – from Roma – from Arretium?

Perhaps it was my destiny from birth. I was named Procula, from the word procul, meaning far, distant, remote. Did my parents give me that odd name because both were so far from their childhood homes – my mother, Roma, and my father, the Alpes region?

Now I, too, have wandered across the Roman Empire – so far away that my name matches my life.

Chapter II

Arretium, where I was born, was located north of Roma in the center of Italia. It was one of the twelve communities of the historic Etruscan Federation, founded centuries ago. It ruled Roma for a hundred years. Artifacts show that the Etruscans were more cultured than their conquerors. Their artisans created the famed bucchero Nero, black ware, some six centuries ago.

When the empire expanded, tile was needed everywhere. Clay was plentiful, so bricks, pipes and conduits were produced for continual projects like long aqueducts, tunnels and roads so Arretium always prospered. Although Roma liked to ignore this, the late great statesman *Caius Maecenas – one of Emperor Augustus' most trusted advisers – came from Arretium. I was proud of my birthplace.

Arretium was also noted for red-glazed tableware, an export that the Roman government encouraged. Many potters were freedmen, but even slaves who copied Greek designs were considered prized artisans. Some had their own distinctive stamps and proudly marked their work. My father laughed that Arretium tilemakers would always have work because Romans built so many bathhouses.

As a young man, my father traveled from the northern Alpes region to learn about tile production. I absorbed some of his adventurous spirit through his old tales of kings and ogres in the great dark forest where his ancestors had lived. After he met my mother, he decided to stay in Arretium. When some kiln owners formed a guild, they asked his advice. Eventually, he became manager for their expanding exports. Once, I found some unique red-glazed cups from Arretium in a Jerusalem marketplace. I bought a dozen just to enjoy looking at something from my hometown.

My mother was never well. She met my father when she was sent by her wealthy family to the northern hill country to escape Roma's summer heat. She became ill on the journey and stopped at Arretium. There, she stayed with a banker's family. By the time summer had passed, she was in love with my father. She married and stayed there. At least, that was the story she told me. Now I believe there was another reason – an earlier relationship – so that her parents discouraged her return to Roma.

Usually, my mother was silent about her past. Sometimes she mentioned a beautiful domus in Roma. Her imperial blood came from the Claudii ancestral line. No doubt, she married beneath her social class. We never visited relatives, nor did any come to see us.

My mother died when I was seven. I remember her lying in a darkened room, holding my face in her hands and kissing my forehead. She let me hold my new-born sister, at first so pink and warm. Then both closed their eyes forever. Each spring my father and I placed Lilia at the underground tomb where they were buried. A local artist did a small fresco on the tomb's walls. It depicted a musician with his double flute and a swaying dancer. The music and dance that illuminated the walls also provided me some solace. Still, the face of my dead sister haunted me for a long time.

My father never spoke about his loss but hugged me daily before I went to school. Girls were better educated in Arretium than in Roma – a fact ignored by my Roman relatives. My father always stopped his work to quiz me when I returned from classes. We were devoted to each other and the household slaves were devoted to our needs. I remember my childhood as an untroubled life.

One early memory remains of my first love. When I was five years old, I watched Guiseppi, a fine young potter, work at his wheel with the easy grace of an athlete. He shaped the wet gray clay with his agile hands as his foot moved the spinning wheel. Smooth shapely vases and bowls emerged from his stand. A lock of black curly hair fell over his forehead as he concentrated on his work. I thought he was as handsome as a Caesar's son although I had no idea of how a Caesar's son looked.

Guiseppi would hand me small pieces of clay which I formed into little animals like odd-shaped zebras even if I had never seen any. My cows were complete with udders. Dogs and cats had elongated tails. One day, I announced that when I grew up, I would marry him.

"Of course, I will marry you, Procula," Guiseppi laughed, "and we will live in a castle-by-the-sea."

However, in spring – when the birds were flying – Guiseppi married his dark-haired sweetheart. I was heartbroken. His bride said that I could come to supper with them the very next week.

Guiseppi swept me up in his arms and added, "I am only a poor potter. Someday, Procula, you'll live in a castle-by-the-sea with a real prince."

At least half of his prediction came true.

I was eleven on that fateful day when I came home from school and found our servants weeping. My father had been killed as he checked the inventory on an outgoing shipment. A wagon, too heavily loaded, toppled over and he was caught in the chaos. He died instantly.

The next days were a blur. My father was buried beside my mother in the family tomb. I didn't know what would happen to me. Our Cook comforted me as best she could. Three days later, a tall stranger arrived and told me he was my avunculus – Zio Ammonius, my mother's brother.

He and his assistant, Lucius, had arrived in an impressive carriage. How the neighbors gawked and whispered! The curtains were drawn, so rumors spread about golden cups and damask pillows inside. Indeed, the pillows were soft to cushion our ride, but I didn't see any golden cups until we reached Roma.

"Procula," my uncle announced abruptly, "you will return with us to Roma. You will live with your aunt, Zia Terentia, and me at Domum Fontana." He added in a stern voice, "You're a very fortunate young girl that we are willing to give you a home."

I tried not to be fearful since he was my only uncle, but from the beginning I felt a certain wariness. For one thing, he seldom looked directly at me. He always gazed above my head or out of the window, as if he didn't want to see me. He tilted back his large head with a slight gesture to suggest his hawk-like nose smelled an offending odor. Did he suspect that I would interfere with his well-ordered life? It was a fleeting thought that I would use later. I could irritate him with a feigned innocence. I knew I was smarter than he suspected.

Zio Ammonius stood erect. His height and manner made him an impressive figure, easily recognized as a member of the aristocratic honestiores class. That meant he had a million sesterces and provided some public service by sponsoring a few arena games. His firm jaw jutted out from a long neck. His gray hair was cropped close. His mouth remained firm and serious. Later, I realized that he seldom smiled at his family. I saw from his narrowed eyelids and piercing black eyes a resentment over my presence.

21

However, he always acted as a genial host, greeting anyone else with a warm Ave amicus!

Zio's cloak was of finest gray wool. A golden band encircled his upper arm. On one hand, he wore a large cameo of Emperor Caesar Augustus. A second golden ring bore his own insignia to imprint documents. His large hands quickly grasped my father's will even before it was offered. He stroked his head as if deep in thought. "Procula will return with us to Roma in the morning!" he announced. "My word is law!"

Cook protested, "Are you sure it's the right. . .?" and then stopped. So, my trunk was packed with clothes, an inlaid box of my mother's jewelry, a few scrolls, and my father's Mithras god, a terra cotta statue. My father never celebrated Mithras Day on December twenty-fifth. Probably, the little idol was some potter's sample that he viewed as an art object. My father really followed the Greek practice of a Stoic, accepting whatever came without complaint. Usually, I followed his example. No more. With luck and cunning I would change my uncle's plans for me. I would stay in Arretium.

Early that morning, Cook came to my uncle. "Sir," she said with a respectful nod, "now that my husband and I have been granted our freedom, we could keep the house and take care of Procula until she marries . . ."

Zio Ammonius raised his eyebrows in disdain. "Stay here? In Arretium? Never! As the only child of my late sister, I am her legal guardian. Her future is secure with me."

Cook stood her ground. "Don't take her away from the only home she's known."

"She will have advantages in Roma that will benefit everyone," he sniffed. "My sister married beneath her class. I'll see that doesn't happen to Procula."

That ended the conversation. Lucius took my hand and guided me to the carriage. As two sleek steeds responded to the driver's whip, I turned to wave to the servants. Cook wiped her eyes and, trembling, I waved back.

"What will happen to them?" I asked.

Zio Ammonius frowned at me. In an irritated voice, he grumbled, "Your father decreed in his will that they should be set free. Such foolishness! When I think what they would bring in Roma . . ."

Lucius gave me a sympathetic look. During negotiations with the tile management, I wondered about Lucius who was not a slave, yet always a step behind my uncle. He accommodated Zio Ammonius with stylus and ink as my uncle signed documents and wrapped up my father's business affairs.

Lucius had a regal bearing, an inner self-assurance that gave him dignity and authority when he walked into a room. He was of medium height, dark-skinned, and wore a flowing saffron robe marked by a jet-black geometric design. His black and tan striped turban was centered with a topaz stone that glistened in the sunlight. Exotic as a foreign prince, it was hard not to stare at him. His quick brown eyes measured every movement, every word. Occasionally, my uncle depended on Lucius' knowledge. Lucius also carried a leather pouch with the diploma, a passport which allowed my uncle certain privileges in travel. It also conveyed to others that my uncle was someone of great importance. Lucius' hands were smooth and soft. I felt comforted by his gentle touch.

When the carriage pulled away, I didn't look back. My father's servants were fortunate to stay in Arretium. Even at eleven, I knew that while I was not a slave, I certainly was not free. In my head, I formed a plan to return to Arretium. I would scheme. I would be victorious.

Zio Ammonius was seated so he could view the passing scenery. Lucius and I sat together with our backs against the driver's rack. Moved with emotion and the swaying carriage, I felt queasy. I wiped away a few tears with the back of my hand while Zio Ammonius avoided looking at me.

Lucius put a cushion in his lap. He arranged the folds of his robe and then motioned to me. "If you're tired, you can rest here."

I slumped down beside him. The pillow felt cool on my cheek. I closed my eyes and hoped when I opened them, the carriage would have a broken axle and we would return to Arretium. It was a childish wish.

I pretended to sleep. That was a talent that I had perfected. I found it very useful at times. I could overhear conversations, as well as avoid household tasks. I felt Lucius brush away a curl that fell across my cheek.

"She's rather a beautiful child . . . much like her mother," he said.

". . . Except for the auburn hair and fair skin. That's what comes from marriage with northerners." Zio Ammonius paused. "My sister was so angry at being sent away that summer that she never came back." He hesitated again. "It had nothing to do with you, Lucius. It was just that she was young. Through our clan, she was of the Claudii family. We had to protect the ancestral line."

". . . And I was a slave at the time." There was a hard edge in Lucius' voice.

"Our parents were sure she would get over her infatuation . . ."

". . . Which she did. She married the tile-maker and I bought my freedom. So, everything worked out well for everyone, didn't it?"

Zio Ammonius slapped his knee. "It didn't work out so well for me. I've had to pay you a handsome salary since you've become so wise and shrewd!"

"Get rid of me then! I'll go to your enemies and tell them everything I know about your bank!" Lucius bantered back.

"I can't do that," Zio Ammonius countered. "How could I manage without you? You are too clever. You know that, and I know that. Besides, I really need you now. You must help me with Terentia when we show up with Procula. My wife has a very difficult time when our sons come home on vacation! They interrupt her time with her friends. Now, she won't be happy to oversee Procula, who is really a stranger."   Lucius responded, "If Terentia adopts Procula as one of the family, she can wear the special dress, the honoredius trium liberorum, as the mother of three children."

"That's another of Emperor Augustus' awful laws to strengthen the family! With three children a wife is granted freedom from her husband's decisions! No, don't suggest the adoption of Procula to Terentia." Zio Ammonius snapped, "It will only make her more independent and bring me more trouble!"

"Procula's father was very astute in business," Lucius continued. "She has a fine fortune from him, and with her mother's dowry . . ."   Fortune? Dowry? Though my eyes were closed, I was instantly alert. My father had never mentioned money to me. We always lived very comfortably, so I had no need to know of my father's business affairs. He always gave me spending money that I kept in a hidden waistline pouch.

"That was a surprise," Zio Ammonius answered. "Since my sister was ill, I expected that her dowry would have disappeared. You know how women are. My wife's dowry was spent long ago, but then Terentia has extravagant taste." He gave a rueful laugh. "It keeps me motivated to increase my own holdings! I think I'll invest Procula's fortune in property, rather than a shipping partnership. There's a stunning view on the seacoast beyond Lavinium that interests me. If her dowry was invested in that land and I built a villa there, it would be beneficial for everyone."

Lucius said slowly, "Maybe Procula won't like the sea. Terentia doesn't."

"Terentia always goes to her country villa when Roma gets hot in the summer. I prefer the seaside. It's the only place where I can relax. Coastal property will always be a wise investment. I like the idea," Zio Ammonius said with finality.

"Remember. . . Procula's money needs to be easily available when she marries."

Zio Ammonius replied, "I've already given her marriage some thought . . ."

Marry? I don't want to marry anyone. I want to go back to Arretium!   I kept quiet with my eyes closed. I felt like crying, but I needed to hear my uncle's plans and more about my aunt.

Lucius seemed surprised. "I know marriages are arranged at early ages, but still she seems so young."

My uncle sounded like he was discussing a bank transaction. "It depends. Of course, she'll be introduced as part of our family, but she isn't Roman. To have come from Arretium isn't the greatest credential. Her manners . . ."

"She appears to be a well-bred quiet child."

". . . But can she learn the refinements, the etiquette, the fashions of Roma? Even with tutors, it may be too late for her to overcome her provincial habits," Zio Ammonius sighed. "Well, in three years, she'll be fourteen. Then, we'll decide arrangements. Yes, an early marriage for Procula will solve the problem of what to do with her. Marriage is a good solution for everyone."

For everyone except me. I kept my eyes closed. A plan formed in my mind. He was a large man who was always right. Soon I would prove him wrong.

Chapter III

It seemed the carriage clattered along for several hours before we reached our first rest stop. Stone markers along the way indicated the distance to the next town. Every ten miles astatio was built where travelers could stop for fresh horses. After thirty miles, a mansio offered food and lodging. Sometimes, a brothel was located nearby. I had to wait for that first place before I could execute my plan.

A small community surrounded the mansio. There were stables and a blacksmith to shod the horses. A cheese-maker and miller were located on the nearby creek the place was perfect for my scheme – to find a ride back to Arretiuim before my uncle discovered my disappearance.

Zio Ammonius quickly entered the mansio.

"Come along, Procula," Lucius beckoned. "We'll have something to eat."

"I'm not hungry. My stomach gets upset when I ride in a coach. I'll just look at the horses."

Lucius hesitated. "Well, stay nearby. Your uncle always naps a bit after he eats. So, we won't leave for an hour. I'll join you when I'm finished."

He went inside, and I rushed toward the stables. I saw a young man unload a haycart. I didn't hesitate.

"Are you going north toward Arretium?" I asked.

Some stable-hands stopped watering the horses and looked at me. I saw their curious glances.

"Why?" asked the driver. "

My uncle let me ride this far. He's going on to Roma. He wants me to find a ride back to Arretium," I lied.

"Are you sure?"

"Oh, yes!" I pulled out my money pouch. "I have money to pay you." I counted out my money and then handed the pouch to him. "Is that enough?"

He smiled, "Well, I guess I could drive to Arretium for that. Hop up here."

The stable-hands yelled out, "Ask him if he knows the way. The cart might break down. You might need more than money to get there." My cheeks reddened, but I ignored their laughter. Someone helped me up on the wagon seat. I thanked him and didn't look back. I knew that by evening I would be back in Arretium where Cook would smother me with hugs and kisses.

The driver snapped his whip and our cart lumbered away. Roman roads were well-built, so the village was soon behind us. Perhaps we had gone two miles, when we came to a shrine beside the road. It was for Ceres, the goddess of grain.

The driver stopped the horse. "We must honor Ceres," he said. "I'll stay in the cart. You must pay homage in bare feet. Take off your sandals. You must honor her with grain."

It seemed an odd custom, but I gathered up some leftover straw for the shrine. I took off my sandals and jumped down.

"Put the hay at Ceres feet," the driver said. "Close your eyes. Just say a long prayer for a fine harvest this year . . . yes, a fine harvest . . . for me," he laughed, fingering the money pouch that I had given him. I jumped down and walked over to the statue. I closed my eyes, unsure of how to pray to a goddess of grain. As I concentrated, I heard the whip crack. The cart clattered away down the road. I ran after it. "Wait!" I yelled as the cart disappeared into the trees. I slumped down beside the road. I had been duped. I realized that the stable hands knew what would happen. I cried great sobbing tears. If I went back to the mansio, I faced ridicule and anger. I wiped my face on my gown. I held my head high even though some stones cut my feet as I started back to Arretium. I would show everyone!

I'd gone a short distance when I heard a commotion behind me. There was a small cart with a driver and Lucius.

"Get in!" Lucius ordered. "Just where do you think you're going?" "I want to go back to Arretium!"

"We'll talk about that later. You've made your uncle very angry. He was ready to leave you here." Lucius stared hard at me. "Once I ran away when I was a slave. I was beaten and burned with a brand." He pulled up his gown. Ugly scars remained on his legs. "You're lucky that you aren't a slave." He bent over, "I will help you, Procula. Someday . . . if you still wish . . . you can return to Arretium. However, you must come with me now."

I climbed in beside Lucius and we returned in silence to the mansio. Zio Ammonius was already in the carriage.

"I'm sorry," I murmured.

He looked hard at me. "You have delayed me by your silly and selfish act. Time is money! Someday, you may learn that." He stared at my bare feet. "So... you've lost your sandals . . . and money, too? Get in and don't speak until we reach Roma!"

I nodded and fought any tears. Trembling, I kept my head down like an obedient slave. My uncle sighed and looked away. Lucius, silent, was deep in thought. My uncle tapped the roof and the horses clip-clopped in steady rhythm. toward the great capitol.

Along the way, I fantasized about being warmly welcomed in Roma. I pictured my aunt, drawn to me in kinship and sympathy. She would greet me with open arms, a reassuring hug, and a broad smile. Maybe a young slave would show me around the house and gardens since my cousins were away at school. I would be happy in spite of my uncle. I glanced at Lucius and he gave me a small reassuring smile. I relaxed and smoothed my gown. I slept some. At each mansio, Lucius kept me by his side to prevent another escape. We arrived in Roma in late afternoon as dusk settled over the city.

Lucius leaned forward and pointed toward a wall. "That marks a place where the great Servius Tullius built his moat and barricade."

My uncle raised his eyebrows. "The child won't know about Servius Tullius . . ."

"Oh, but I do!" I broke in, anxious for his approval. "He was the sixth king of Roma, who was put on the throne by his mother Tanaquil. She . . ."

Zio Ammonius raised his hand to stop me. "That's enough. We know the story." He gave a deep sigh, bored with my chatter.

I thought Lucius wanted to laugh, but he quickly turned to the window. "Some wonderful gardens are over there. You'll also find the Campus Martius with the theaters of Balbus and Pompey," he added. "My father read all the great plays to me. We often went to the theater," I added proudly.

Lucius nodded approval, but Zio Ammonius only turned away with raised eyebrows. "Roma's theaters have much finer productions than any you have seen."

I kept quiet even though Arretium had traveling companies present Greek dramas all the time.

We rode past homes with brick and stucco exteriors. Some were two stories tall, but most were more simple dwellings. I thought of various terra cotta plaques that were created in Arretium. These homes would be enhanced with some artistic pieces beside their double doors.

We didn't drive into the heart of Roma but turned to the Palatine hills which competed with the Capitoline hills – as I was to find out – for the greatest number of palaces and temples. Later, I discovered that my aunt always identified her friends as "She's a Capitoline" or "She's a Palatine" –a habit which amused me.

I guessed from my uncle's limited conversation and Lucius' manner that Zio Ammonius was very wealthy. However, I was unprepared for the grand domus that awaited us in Roma. Two iron gates were opened by a gatekeeper and we clattered into a courtyard, complete with a marble fountain of two boys holding urns, like Remus and Romulous, the twins who founded Roma centuries ago. A pedestal with a bust of Jupiter stood beside the door to ward off the evil spirits of lying, stealing and drunkenness. Later I would learn that Jupiter was very ineffective at Domum Fontana.

The gatekeeper bowed low to Zio Ammonius and Lucius. He helped me from the carriage with a questioning look. Finally, a small smile lit his face. "Everyone wants to meet you."

Zio Ammonius strode ahead toward the heavy metal doors, now opened as servants and slaves came to stand in line, nod and bow to their master.

Breathlessly, I followed behind Lucius and entered a reception hall with a floor of marble mosaic patterned with signs of the Zodiac. The servants hurried silently away through a side passageway as the paneled doors before us were flung open. I followed the two men into the atrium. Beyond was a peristylium, an open-air courtyard with another fountain in creamy marble. It was stunning – a half-draped Venus, eyes downcast modestly, while sprays of water played at her feet.

There wasn't time to stare, for we crossed the atrium and a recessed covered area to yet another reception room, one of several. A sloping floor in the second court led to a small pool, so rainwater would drain into it from the open area. The floor was edged by beige, rust and black mosaic tiles, centered by a circular design of colorful fruits and leaves. I was taken to a side room, my aunt's personal retreat.

PROCULA | Marion H. Youngquist

Zia Terentia was seated regally on a chair amid flickering oil lamps and huge urns of Lilia. Immediately, I knew this indicated that our meeting was serious. If she had been reclining on a lounge as most people, she would have been relaxed and put me at ease. Instead, she looked at me much as our cook in Arretium would have studied a lamb shank. Her eyes riveted on my bare feet. She shook her head and gave me a pained look.

"So, this is. . . is. . . what is your name?"

"Procula." If my aunt didn't remember my name, did she even know I was coming?

"Of course." Zia Terentia raised her eyebrows. "Come closer. Let me look at you."

I moved forward. She didn't extend her hand or give me the welcoming hug that I so desired.

Zio Ammonius dropped a kiss on his wife's cheek and gave a great sigh. "It was a difficult trip. A carriage ride doesn't improve with distance." He turned to me. "Your aunt will tell you about all the arrangements for your stay." He looked at his wife. "I want a bath immediately, and a massage. I'll eat in the Library by myself tonight." He quickly left. Lucius had already disappeared.

I looked around, desperate to make a good impression. A marble-topped table was on the opposite wall. It was centered with a black vase, etched with red and white markings. I recognized it immediately and rushed toward the table.

"You have a vase . . . a vase from Arretium!"

Zia Terentia cried out, "Stop! Don't touch that! It's an antique Grecian urn – very old! Irreplaceable! No one touches that. . . not even my own slave."

I jumped back. But as I looked at it again, I saw the double rim at the top. I wanted to laugh out loud. I knew the potter who made the vase. In fact, he told me that he had an arrangement with a merchant in Roma who sold his ware as Genuine Greek Antiquities. The Romans envied and copied the Greeks in learning and the arts. It gave me a special thrill that I was superior to Zia Terentia in my knowledge of a fake copy! I had a secret weapon – the Truth! But I kept quiet. For now, I was at her mercy.

She and I ate together that night, mostly in an uncomfortable silence, punctuated by her deep sighs. Occasionally, she would ask a direct question – how many slaves did your father own? Three. How many rooms in your house? Seven. Did he have a villa in the country? No. Have you ever been to school? Yes, since I was seven. And I had a private tutor because my father thought history and geometry were so important.

At this, Zia Terentia sniffed. "That's such an odd idea. Educating girls. . . . so typical of provincial attitudes in the north. Here in Roma, we're much more practical. You'll learn the art of running a household!"

She didn't elaborate. I remembered my father saying, "The Romans build great roads and bridges and aqueducts, but Greeks are the real thinkers." How many bridges would I have to build before I could reach the heart of Zia Terentia?

Our stilted conversation gave me a chance to study her. With quick glances, I saw a short, rather dumpy woman. Her heavy make-up followed the latest trend of dark penciled eyes and a powdered face – a legacy from the famed Cleopatra who lived a half-century ago. AEgyptian fashions had survived and were copied by the Romans. Zia Terentia's jet black hair occasionally took on the reddish hue of a henna rinse. I guessed that she was a proud lady, preoccupied with her own appearance. She had eyes only for herself. When I admired her taste in clothes and jewelry, I gained her approval. Finally, the meal and questions were over.

There were at least fifty rooms at Domum Fontana. Many were grand with painted scenes on the walls. I learned that Zia Terentia frequently had them cleaned and retouched because smoke from the oil lamps darkened them.

I wanted to stay in my mother's room. However, Zia Terentia called a servant to take me, instead, to a room next to the servant quarters. At eleven, the placement was not lost on me. I realized I was not a servant, but neither was I a full member of the family. I was angry. In my room, I planned ways to retaliate. Zia Terentia centered her table with full blown roses. How convenient! Slyly, I could place a wiggly worm to fall from the petals into her honey pot. She might even scream. I hoped she was the screaming kind. If she had a servant girl switched for such oversight, I would offer the slave an extra sweet bun in a sympathetic gesture.

I thought hard. I could slip in and out of rooms easily enough. Soon Zia Terentia would find some frogs in her bedroom. I would trail sand across the atrium floor as I brought her my gift of a sand sculpture. I could even stumble and drop it in her lap. Was it possible to stuff big rose thorns in her litter pillows? Such naughtiness intrigued me. Later, I was secretly pleased to cause a quarrel between my aunt and uncle. She suspected my pranks and wanted to send me away. Zio Ammonius would not hear of it.

"No! I have plans for Procula," he snapped. "You never controlled our sons. Procula should be easier. Girls have simple minds. Find something for her to do!" He stormed out of the room.

When I became an adult, I received compliments about how graciously I welcomed strangers. I always remembered that first night and my aunt's cold reception.

Etiam sanato volnere cicatrix manet – After the wound is healed, the scar remains.

Chapter IV

On my first morning, an older woman awakened me. She was thin with prominent hard muscles on her slim arms. Blue veins webbed her agile hands. Her gray hair was in a twisted bun. In all, she appeared neat and tidy, but a conspicuous hump on her back was obvious. However, her eyes were kind and the hazel glints in them added to her unusual appearance. She carried a tray with fruit and bread, and a glass of milk.

"I'm called Weaver. Eat up and wash yourself clean before we go to your aunt." She handed me a soft towel – perhaps the softest I'd ever felt – and turned to leave the room. "Be sure to wear clean clothing."   I ate slowly, amused that Weaver would tell me what to wear. Did this household in Roma think I was so ignorant that I wouldn't be clean and properly dressed?

It was late in the morning before we went to Zia Terentia. Her personal slave was fixing Zia Terentia's black hair in the Grecian style of curls around her face with a knot crowning her head. A silver mirror and inlaid ivory combs were beside a tray of glittering rings. Several were heavy gold, set with sparkling stones. One was coiled like a tiny snake with emerald pinpoint eyes. My aunt was intent, choosing a ring for every finger. She took them on and off. She lifted her hand and waved each ring to catch the light. She considered everyone carefully. It was like a choreographed dance.

PROCULA | Marion H. Youngquist

I was fascinated by her quick frowns and quicker smile over each choice. Carefully, her slave painted my aunt's lips and lined her eyes. With arched eyebrows, Zia Terentia began her instructions as she sipped a goblet of red wine.

"Procula, you must realize that I'm extremely busy. The demands upon my time are endless." She gave a deep sigh. "Already this morning, Lucius has dealt with the hawkers beyond the courtyard. They wish to sell us rugs . . . perfumes . . . nuts . . . only the finest things. Roman merchants want our business. They love to sell to this household. Then I must approve all of Lucius' decisions." She gave me a stern look. "You will realize, as you get older, how important this address is. You're very fortunate to live here."

I lowered my eyes and hoped that I nodded humbly enough. I looked at Weaver, bent and impassive. Our eyes were almost at the same level.

Zia Terentia rattled on, ". . . I am placing you under the direction of Weaver here. She knows the household well. She designs and makes all of our linens. My household is famous for its linens. You must learn how to run a household. You'll have your own to supervise someday."

I felt a slight chill. Maybe she means to marry me off sooner rather than later. Angry, I fingered a small mirror of Zia Terentia's. As she reached for it, I dropped it. Jagged pieces lay at her feet.

"Clumsy girl!" she snapped. "Don't touch anything of mine again!" She took a deep breath. "Now . . . where was I? Oh, yes . . . the supervision of a household. You must learn to choose things of quality and good taste. I would be embarrassed if any young woman under my influence would do otherwise." In between sentences, she continued to drink until her glass was empty. "Of course, I have sons, but I suppose I will have to train their wives, too. One never knows. . . even with good blood lines." She added with a large burp, "Now run along, and don't bother the servants."

At this, I was dismissed. I knew I was to stay out of Zia Terentia's sight. I was relieved that Weaver was there to take me away – and curious how she and I would get along. I followed her to the slaves' compound. In a second-floor room, there were large looms, a table, a long bench, two spinning wheels, stools, and several shelves with spindles of brightly colored thread. One loom held white material with a black Greek Key design along the edge. Two swarthy slave women deftly moved shuttles back and forth at other looms.

Weaver looked at me. "Now. . . what do you want to do?"

I wanted to leave a mouse in my aunt's bed, but – even more – I really wanted to go back to Arretium. I said, "I want to go home."

Weaver considered this. "Some things are impossible."

I started to cry. Weaver sat down beside me and handed me a soft cloth. "Here . . . wipe your eyes. I know what it is to leave a home. Someday, you may even like living here. Your aunt is not a hard woman . . . just insensitive. I've known her for many years. We are distant cousins. I had a bent back and no dowry. I would have become a beggar, but she took me in and saw that I learned the loom. Of course, I'm a slave, but in this house, we eat very well, and we're warm in winter. Sometimes, I'm invited to her country estate in the summer. Oh, life could be much worse."

She sounded like another Stoic. I was lucky. I didn't have a bent back. I wasn't a slave. I could bear living here also – for a while.

Then she added those dreaded words, "Besides, sometime soon, you'll be married."

"I don't want to get married."

"Ah, you will be lucky. You have a large dowry."

There was that word – dowry– again. Was I wealthy like my uncle and aunt?

". . . And they will see that you have a fine husband and from a wealthy family, too."

Marriage and money – that seemed my future. Weaver turned to her loom with deft fingers. I watched her closely. She didn't like my scrutiny. She suggested that I look at the gardens. So, I left.

The gardens delighted me, especially one stone loggia at the end of a languid pool. Pale lotus blossoms floated on the surface. Beyond the pool, tall cypresses stood like sentinels. It seemed there were many places to enjoy, so I went to my room and returned with a scroll. I read until Weaver came searching for me at mealtime. That afternoon she insisted that I read to her while she was weaving. So, my life began at Domum Fontana. I was considered a quiet child because I stayed out of everyone's way.

Perhaps I will always regard my first year with mixed emotions. Days fell into a pattern. Daily, we attended the public baths. The Romans insisted on cleanliness. I played games with slave children, although my aunt disapproved. I visited libraries. Many in Roma were connected with the baths and temples. I loved finding a private corner to read an exciting historical tale. I listened to lectures.

I dreamed of running away, but where would I go? Zio Ammonius said that Cook and her husband had returned to the Alpes region. I needed money to escape. My uncle controlled my inheritance. Once I slashed his money pouch, so his coins spilled out. When I considered living forever in Roma with my uncle and aunt, my days seemed bleak. At times, I scarcely ate. Then the Baker would persuade me to eat his crusty warm bread with a dish of white grated cheese and herbed olive oil for dipping.

Fall, winter and spring were spent at Domum Fontana. However, in the summer I went with Weaver and Zia Terentia (along with her personal slaves) to the country. The property had been in Zia Terentia's family for

PROCULA | Marion H. Youngquist

several generations. I found a stray kitten for a pet. I called it Cicero and the estate, The Farm. My aunt quickly corrected me.

"Villa Fortunata is an important country estate . . . one of the largest. It is not a farm!" she snapped.

I stumbled against her as she held a glass of wine. It spilled down the front of her peach silk stola. Quickly, I turned to get help and bumped a pedestal stand with a bowl of roses. It fell over and the bowl shattered. Those mistakes were real accidents.

"Get out! Play with your cat!" Zia Terentia ordered. "Don't help anyone!"

I fled in tears. Broken glass was a bad omen. Was trouble my destiny? Daily, I lived in fear. It helped that life at Villa Fortunana was simpler-- more like Arretium. We stayed for the two hottest months. Zio Ammonius occasionally came, but he spent more time building his new villa on the coast with a view of Mare Tuscum. Zia Terentia didn't take any interest in his project. She disliked the sea.

"How can I sleep with the crashing waves and noisy gulls?" she complained.

Later, I went to the seaside with Lucius. I dipped my toes in the sea and hunted shells. Zio Ammonius wanted a special hanging woven for his great hallway, so I also went with Weaver to view the space. I remember large and airy rooms with curved ceilings and wide balconies.

While I played along the shore, Zio Ammonius stood beside me, gazing at his fine new residence. "Procula, I hope you realize that this villa will be yours someday." He was in an expansive mood. "I've invested your dowry in this property, so you will have a home when you marry." He also meant that I couldn't spend my own money.

I gasped. "Mirabele visu!" meaning "It is wonderful to behold."

"That's it!" he exclaimed. "We'll call it Villa Mirabele. Now. . . what would you like in it?"

If he meant furnishings, I didn't care. Or did he mean a husband?

I held up a pearly pink shell. "This. I want lots of shells."

Zio Ammonius laughed, "You shall have them."

The next time I visited Villa Mirabele, I saw a shell motif carved over doors and in the paneling. Although it wasn't a castle, I wondered if this villa was my future castle by-the-sea that Guiseppi had foretold. Again, I was wrong.

Chapter V

As I grew older, I realized that the wealth of Zia Terentia and Zio Ammonius also allowed them to live in two separate worlds. For many rich Romans, marriage was an arrangement to unite prominent families and protect their fortunes and prestige. I knew my parents had been different and lived lovingly together.

I met my cousins – Julius and Octavianus, named for the two Caesars – when they came home from school in Pompeii, south of Roma. I wondered why they were living away from Roma with its fine schools. As I later realized, the wealthy sent their arrogant sons to distant towns, so tutors – usually Greeks – could deal with their recklessness. My cousins barely noticed me those first two summers.

Emperor Caesar Augustus, who was called Octavianus in childhood, died at the age of seventy-six. People were uneasy. Who would lead and inspire the Empire? His great projects had meant high employment and even higher spending. The Romans loved their costly imported luxuries – oriental silks, Egyptian gems, far-eastern ivory, pungent spices, parchment, perfumes, nuts, and rare woods. Traders flocked to Roma to sell their wares. Unfortunately, Roma's exports were mainly limited to wine and pottery.

Zio Ammonius complained about an imbalance of trade and worried about his future financial situation. He said that too many young men shunned military service, so foreign mercenaries filled the army posts. Family life declined from poor relationships. Even Emperor Augustus exiled his daughter, Julia, to an island because of her affairs. Zia Terentia said the Romans never quite forgave him for his harsh treatment.

"She was young. Does marriage make anyone faithful?" Aunt Terentia shrugged.

I copied Zio Ammonius and honored the Emperor as our Messiah, our Savior of the world, believing his reign had brought prosperity and peace – Pax Romana. Although Augustus built over eighty great marble temples, religion didn't inspire any deep feeling or godly awe. It was empty of all humility or hope. Military might create an empire around the great sea which made power more important than any spiritual goodness.

Zia Terentia announced that Julius and Octavianus would return from Pompeii as they were among the young people chosen to chant the lament for the dead at Augustus' cremation. After that honor, she never let her friends forget that her sons were part of those ceremonies at the Field of Mars.

I reread my history book, determined not to be ignorant of our glorious past or be scorned by my cousins. It was good that I enjoyed reading, as it was wasted time as far as they were concerned. When they returned, they pursued their friends and attended the chariot races at the Circus Maximus. Any history was dismissed as being of no worth.

Julius was the older. Already seventeen, he was as tall as Zio Ammonius and wore his dark hair curled in the latest fashion – a crown of ringlets. His eyes seemed to mock others, even his mother, and I sensed he felt superior to anyone around him.

"So, our little cousin is growing up," he remarked, drawing me into a firm embrace, ". . . and so enchanting! Should I share you with Roma or keep you hidden?"

I giggled – somewhat nervously. His arm remained around my shoulders.

Zia Terentia reminded me, "We're having a special banquet tonight to honor the return of Julius and Octavianus. So, Procula, you must be on your best behavior."

I started to move from Julius' embrace, but his hand swiftly ran down my back. I felt a hard pinch when he reached my buttocks.

Instinctively, I jumped. "O-o-o-w."

A smirking Julius walked away.

Zia Terentia turned to me. "Whatever is the matter now?"

"Nothing. . . nothing at all. I thought I saw a spider." It was a lame lie.

Zia Terentia was irritated. "Honestly, Procula, use some self-control! Whatever will Julius' friends think if a silly spider sets you off?"

38

PROCULA | Marion H. Youngquist

I fled to my room. Julius had made a bold gesture and even on the threshold of womanhood, I recognized a male signal of power. What liberties would he take with me – his young cousin – if we were alone? My dream of a close-knit loving family ended. The next day Julius found his favorite sandals floating in the well. Ha! I knew nothing! I hoped Octavianus would be my true friend as he was only two years older than I. Soon that hope faded, too, as I found Octavianus couldn't be trusted either. He had a talent for slyness and deception behind his beefy moon-face appearance.

Sometimes, Lucius would press a coin in my hand if I went with Weaver to the shops. I seldom bought anything from street vendors, as there were better treats from the kitchen at Domum Fontana. I deposited my coins in a carved wooden pyx.

Octavianus begged with pouty lips, "Procula, can you loan me a couple of sesterces? I'm going to the races. I'll pay you back tomorrow."

Trusting, I took him to my room and opened my coin box. I handed him the money – even additional coins – when he saw all my savings. He hurried away without even a peasant grazie. When he returned that evening, Octavianus whispered that he'd lost my money.

"Don't tell anyone!" he pleaded. "I promise to get my allowance from Lucius before I start back to school. You'll be repaid."

The next morning, my cousins left early for Pompeii. When I woke up. I asked Lucius if Octavianus had left any money for me. When he heard my story, Lucius repaid the debt.

Chapter VI

I think my childhood ended at that time. First, my trust was shaken by both cousins. Then I wondered why the gods had failed to save our Patriae – the father of our country. I joined in the national rites of mourning for Caesar Augustus. His adopted stepson, Tiberius Claudius Nero Caesar, was our new Emperor. People were wary, since his mother, Livia, intended to share his reign. That meant death to any of their rivals.

"So, Tiberius wants to restore the republic?" Lucius asked with a cynical smile.

". . . A political move," Zio Ammonius observed. "The Senate refused. It knows that Tiberius wields great power. It's true that he refuses titles or to have a month named for him as Julius Caesar and Caesar Augustus allowed. But Tiberius will be quick with the sword if he suspects treason. He is slow of speech, and a sour, stern aristocrat."

"No wonder Tiberius is cynical! He was forced to divorce his own beloved wife and marry Julia, Augustus' daughter. They never loved each other." Lucius added softly, "It is hard to live without love."

"Already Tiberius has halted the building of any new temples. He's decreed no new taxes and no more war. He'll increase the treasury and demand strict accounting records." Zio Ammonius grew thoughtful. "No doubt, he would be happy just to live on an island surrounded by poets and Greek philosophers."

"I hear Sejanus, who is prefect of the Praetorian Guard, has emerged as his trusted protector and advisor. No one sees Tiberius, except with Sejanus' permission. That means trouble, as Sejanus accepts bribes," Lucius added.

I wandered off, tired of their conversation. Emperor Tiberius had nothing to do with my life. Again – how wrong I was.

While my cousins were away at school in Pompeii, I finished growing up – at least in height. I was taller and perhaps a trifle thin by Roman standards.

Lucius stopped me in the garden and said, "You look so much like your mother."

"You knew her? Please . . . tell me about her."

He looked away, remembering the past. "Ah . . . yes. We were both children here. However, I was only a slave. We often played together."

I was confused. ". . . A slave?"

He laughed, "No longer. As a boy, I had a quick, agile mind. Your grandfather found me cleverer at numbers," he corrected himself, ". . . I was almost as clever as your uncle. So, he educated us together. Eventually, I became his younger assistant. He was generous with my wages, and I was able to buy my freedom."

It sounded strange to return money to one's master for freedom. For a long time, I'd heard whispers by the servants about my dowry. But could I buy my freedom even if I could collect my money? Zio Ammonius controlled my life.

"So, you continued to work for my grandfather?"

"I stayed in the household." Again, he didn't meet my eyes. "This had been my home. And your mother . . . the people I knew best . . . lived here."

He walked away. I was filled with a youthful fantasy – a romantic illusion – that my mother and Lucius had a special relationship. I carefully approached the subject with Weaver.

"Did you know my mother?" I asked. "Did she really have a cough when she was sent to the north for her health?"

"Questions! You ask the strangest questions! I never met your mother, but, if she was sent away, it was for good reason. Accept that it was for her health. Let your mother rest in peace and think about your future . . . about the banquet your Zia Terentia is giving. It will be exciting."

For the moment, I accepted her advice. I quit asking questions.

When school was out, Julius went to Alexandria to learn – so he claimed – about shipping partnerships and the banking business. Zia Tarentia dreamed that he would live up to his namesake, the great Julius Caesar, who had stabilized the empire's monetary system by basing it on gold reserves. Did she really believe that Julius' would someday direct the national treasury? She was sure that both Julius and Octavianus would have brilliant futures since their birth stars had been in a right alignment.

A huge banquet was held on Julius' return. Zia Terentia ordered garlands of grapes throughout the house. Great bowls of fruit and flowers decorated the tables as if we were celebrating the feast of Saturnalia. Octavianus came home from Pompeii. Since Julius was the center of attention, the young women flirted with him. His friends greeted him heartily and accepted his accounts of an exciting time in AEgyptus. Octavianus pouted moodily at his brother's popularity and went out to the garden with younger boys, arguing the merits of certain gladiators and charioteers. They made small bets on the upcoming races at Circus Maximus. He hardly spoke to me.

Zia Terentia and Zio Ammonius wanted to retire, allowing the party to continue for the young people. She said to me, "Procula, it's time you learned to take care of things. You must stay up and send the young people on their way tonight."

Perhaps I looked alarmed.

"Lucius will help you with the servants . . . and Julius and Octavianus, too," she added. She left, trailing behind Zio Ammonius.

By now, Julius had drunk a great deal and was growing louder. Lucius signaled a servant to fill Julius' glass with half water. I was tired of the noise and drinking. I wanted the party to end. Finally, the last guest went into the dark night. As the carriages clattered away, slaves rode with their young owners to guard against robberies.

Julius threw a sandal across the courtyard. It landed in a rosebush. "I did impress them, didn't I?"

I nodded and headed for the stairs.

"Well, Procula, say something! Talk to me, my dear cousin!' He grabbed my hand and pulled me down on a couch. "Only, you aren't little anymore." He drew me closer. I struggled to increase the distance between us. "Funny, Procula . . . you are so shy. Don't be afraid of me. We could be great friends. We could even help each other."

"It's been a long evening. I'm going up to bed." I tried to rise, but he firmly held my arm.

"I'm tired too," he continued, slurring his words. "Massage my back!"

"I'm not a slave!"

". . . Or I'll massage your back," he said, moving closer.

At this moment, Lucius moved out of the shadows. "Julius, I've called your slave to help you to bed. You have an appointment tomorrow morning with Senator Lepidus. He wishes to hear about piracy near Alexandria. He values your opinion very highly."

Julius forgot about me. He rose unsteadily, as Lucius put out his hand to assist him. "Really? No doubt he wants me to address the Senate!"

Both Lucius and I had to look away or we would laugh. The idea of Julius speaking to any group of older men was ridiculous. However, I knew his pompous self-confidence would last throughout his life. He would never hear anyone but himself.

Lucius left with Julius and I climbed the stairway to my room. From the upper landing, the stars above the atrium looked especially bright. As I thought about the party, it seemed to improve in retrospect. The flowers, the gardens, the food were all superb. I could even forgive the foolishness of Julius and his tipsy state.

I was startled when Lucius came up behind me. "Procula," he whispered, "things have changed in the household now that Julius and Octavianus are home. I want you to sleep in Weaver's room tonight. She's expecting you to stay there."

"But why?"

Lucius hesitated. "It's better for you not to be alone. There's no lock on your door."

Sometimes what isn't said is more important than what is. I knew he wished to protect me. Foolishly, I felt I was able to take care of myself. After all, I was old enough to go to the baths without Zia Terentia. Sometimes, I even handled the money when I went with Weaver to the market for unusual thread – colored silks or AEgyptian cotton.

"Tomorrow, you must ask your aunt for a slave."

I was stunned. "Me? Have a slave? Whatever for? What would I do with a slave?"

He weighed his words carefully. "She will always be ready to help you."

I thought he meant I was still a child and needed assistance. "I can take care of myself!" I said, with a defiant toss of my head.

Lucius paused and studied me carefully. "Ask your Zia Terentia when Livilla arranges her hair. Tell her that if you are to learn hostess duties, you must know how to command the servants. It will help if you have a slave of your own to train."

Was there another reason for Lucius' proposal? I frowned, "I don't know..."

"A slave can be a friend as well," he continued, adding softly, "... as your mother found me."

"Of course, if you think it best ..."

"Your aunt must think it is your idea. When she asks me about it? I'll support you."

He waited until I had gathered my night things. Weaver was awake and lay on a straw pallet. She pointed to her bed – that I was to use it. It was pointless to protest since she was a servant and I was a family member. My head was spinning with Lucius' suggestion. I knew exactly who I wanted for a slave. I was too excited to sleep.

Chapter VII

From that first day when Zia Terentia had left me to Weaver's supervision, I had shadowed Weaver's daily movements. We formed a duo. I could always sense when she tired of my company. Then, I made an excuse to go to the baths or read in the garden. Or I'd run down and watch the kitchen staff make the daily bread. Sometimes, the baker let me help. More than once I patted the loaves with pride. He showed me how to braid sweet bread and embellish the crust with fruit or leaf shapes. The staff trusted me, as I never told Zia Terentia that they made extra pastries for her parties, so they could enjoy some, too.

On my best days Weaver and I walked to market to see the huge array of goods from faraway provinces. Luxuries came overland from Asia or sometimes on Phoenician boats during the safe sailing months. Along with Zio Ammonius' complaints about an imbalance of trade, he ranted against the amount of grain that was needed to feed the poor. Old slaves and immigrants pouring into Roma were also on the dole. I ignored his warnings. I delighted in the foreign shops and their exotic wares. I liked the variety of peoples, and their strange languages. The sights and sounds of the market were exciting.

When Weaver and I ambled along the street of glass blowers, the colors and shapes fascinated us both. Weaver studied the glass patterns and came back to her loom, trying to recreate swirls instead of the usual rigid geometric patterns. Then she decided to experiment with textures for a small woven rug. She intended to make a sample to use in her own room. If it wore well, a similar one would find its way into the household.

So, we came to the Rug Seller street. Many of these merchants had moved from the outer provinces – Syria, Armenia, and AEgyptus. Some had looms in their shops where family members tied fine knots with nimble fingers. Colorful flowers and animals were created amid intricate patterns.

It was in such a shop that I first saw Tuum. Weaver was busy haggling with the shop owner about the price of pale blue thread. As she pulled it carefully through her fingers, she complained that it had not been spun with an even hand.

Several children were at the looms. I noticed a small girl, crouching down. She was far too young to labor so intently. She turned and stared at me with two luminous dark eyes, like a wounded animal afraid of its captor. I smiled, trying to coax a response. The merchant spoke sharply to her and she turned back to her work, her fingers working faster than before.

"Your daughter has lovely eyes," I said.

"She's not my child! We found her abandoned on the street. My wife thinks she can be taught, but I'm doubtful," he grunted, scowling at her.

Over the next months, Weaver and I were in the shop several times. She liked the variety of the merchant's threads. By now, she found him some-what amiable over prices, so transactions were brief. Each time, I tried to coax a smile from the small girl. She stared back without any emotion. Once when Weaver and the merchant were in a side room, I offered the child nutmeats which I'd bought for her. She looked toward the storage room and stared at me impassively. I was determined to make her smile – to get some emotion, some response from this somber frightened child.

One day I slipped a date, stuffed with a nut, into her hand. As she reached for it, her sleeve fell back, and I saw an ugly welt on her right arm. It made me so ill, I stepped to the shop's entrance for fresh air. Fortunately, she had eaten the date before her master and Weaver returned to the room. Weaver had several green spindles wrapped in a sheet. As I turned back to wave to the injured child, she was focused on her loom with a faint smile. If Lucius could bargain, this little girl would be my slave. I was prepared to argue with Zia Terentia about my choice.

The next morning I came to Zia Terentia Her slave brushed her hair in slow easy strokes, which always had a soothing effect. Had Lucius arranged that?

I took a deep breath. "I have a favor to ask, Zia Terentia."

"Another?"

I tried hard to think of anything I had recently requested. "I'm older now . . . almost fourteen . . . and . . . and . . .," I blurted out, ". . . and I want a slave."

"A slave for you?" Zia Terentia frowned. "Whatever for?"

Her slave gave me a wink and held up her brush.

"My hair . . . it takes so much time to do my hair. . . and there's not enough time for Livilla to do both my hair and yours."

Zia Terentia considered this. "You're so right. That's very thoughtful, Procula."

It was a compliment I didn't expect.

"Of course, the money for your slave will have to come from your dowry. You can't expect us to pay for everything. A slave will be expensive."

"Maybe Lucius can find someone younger," I answered smoothly. "Someone. . . I can practice training."

Zia Terentia looked at me directly. "You can't expect me to help with that either. You'll need Lucius' permission and he'll have to supervise any training. I'm so terribly rushed I can't take on another thing." With her hand, she waved me away.

I met Lucius in the hall. We both wore broad smiles.

It was strange how cheap life really was. Buying a slave became an easy transaction. We rode in litters, side by side. Lucius was dressed in a simple linen toga. His colorful turban was left at home. I marveled at his black shining brow and wondered what secrets he kept in his head, especially when his face was impassive.

I pointed to the shop. "That's it. I hope the child hasn't been sold to someone else."

Lucius stopped and surveyed the area. It was as if he were calculating the merchant's investment and income all at once. "Now . . . Procula, it's unfortunate, but you must say nothing. Leave the bargaining to me."

The Syrian stood in the doorway, inviting prospective customers inside to inspect the finest of rugs, the best of workmanship – for a small price – only available in his shop. He was puzzled to see me, maybe unsure of my relationship with both Weaver and Lucius. I nodded silently, anxious to get inside. Nothing had changed. My waif was crouched on the floor, tying knots of rust wool. The other children were at their looms with agile fingers.

"Salve!" Lucius greeted him. "My young friend here told me about your rugs. I want to see one of medium size."

"I have the best," he beamed. He started to riffle through a pile of rugs in the corner.

I tried to catch the child's eye with a reassuring smile, but she didn't respond. I saw Lucius finger different rugs. I thought he'd never get to our real purpose. "Yes, this rug is very fine . . . very fine. But how would I keep it . . . sweep it? That's work for slaves and children."

The merchant looked at me to see if I would do the work. I shook my head.

Lucius nodded toward me. "It is for her room. Yes, we could buy this if we had someone to sweep it."

The merchant didn't want to lose this sale. "Surely, you can find some-one . . ."

Lucius turned around. "That child . . . there . . . can she sweep a room?"

Beaming, the merchant replied, "Of course! Of course! She's obedient and will do as you ask. A fine worker! A fine worker!" His anxious voice betrayed him.

"Are you willing to sell her?"

"Yes! At a good price . . . a fair price." The merchant pulled the child beside him.

Lucius frowned. "She's too small."

I almost interrupted him, but his stern look silenced me.

"She will grow."

"Then she'll eat too much." Lucius turned away as if any sale was ended. "Feed her on bread and water." "Then she'll be sullen and won't work as hard."

The merchant gave himself away. "If I have trouble with her, I beat her. Oh, she works fast enough with a switch on her back."

I remembered the welts on her thin forearms and closed my eyes in disgust. Lucius and the merchant haggled some more, with Lucius moving toward the door and then back again as if he were rethinking the merchant's deal. Finally, the sale was completed. The rug would be delivered that very afternoon at Domum Fontana. The Syrian raised his eyebrows, pleased and surprised at the address.

"You can have the child," the merchant said, pushing the shy waif toward us. "I have too many mouths to feed with my own seven." He barked something at the child and she hung her head, afraid to look up. She stood behind us in slave fashion.

Once outside, I took her hand. She grasped it so tightly and clung so closely to my side that I knew we were bound together forever.

I turned to Lucius and said, "I didn't ask her name."

Lucius replied, "You own her now. You can call her by any name you wish."

I turned to her. "Your name . . . what's your name?"

A small smile flickered across her brown face and her eyes shone with happiness. She held my hand even tighter. "Tuum est," she grinned, meaning "It is yours" in Latin.

How odd that she referred to herself as aunt — as if she had no name.

I started to repeat, "Tuum . . .?"

She nodded brightly.

So, we called her Tuum and she became mine.

Tuum leaned against me in the litter. Lucius and I planned to sneak her into Domum Fontana before Zia Terentia saw her. Tuum was unkempt, with matted black hair and grimy bare feet. Her hands were clean, so that she wouldn't smudge the rug wool. The Romans believed that the good life started with cleanliness. Neither my aunt or uncle ever missed their daily trips to the public natoriums. Even the slaves took frequent baths.

Lucius and I went off to the merchant in mid-morning when Zia Terentia would be at the Venus baths. It would be a good time to bring Tuum home. However, our plans were spoiled. Zia Terentia had developed a headache — an ailment that had occurred more frequently in the last few months. She was resting in the atrium and wanted to see us immediately. At the sight of Tuum, she turned away in disgust.

"Really, Lucius, what is wrong with you? You certainly could do better than that, even for Procula. Even she needs something more than. . . than that trash!"

I glanced down at Tuum because she was trembling. I knew, then, how intelligent she was. Small as she was, she understood every word of Zia Terentia's outburst. I started to protest, but Lucius interrupted.

"Oh, kind mater," he said smoothly. "She came with the finest rug that Procula could buy today."

Zia Terentia sat up straighter. "Rug? Procula bought a rug?"

"And one so beautiful," I murmured. "The softest blues and reds with a fanciful design of flowers and birds."

My aunt faced Lucius. "Why didn't you buy one for me? Surely, my bedroom needs a new rug, too."

Lucius bowed slightly. "I'll find one for you tomorrow."

Zia Terentia glanced at Tuum again. "Oh, take her away and clean her up." Perhaps the child's dark pleading eyes softened my aunt's heart. "I'll offer a prayer at Fortuna Virilis that you may find a way to conceal her defects." With a wave of her hand, we were dismissed.

I was amused by Zia Terentia's solution. She was a religious woman in many ways. She vacillated between the shrine of the AEgyptian goddess, Isis, and the worship of the Great Mother Cybele. Then she returned to the Temple of Fortuna Virilis when she discovered a few wrinkles. She had great faith that the goddess there might disclose how her defects could be disguised from others – especially men.

Within in an hour, Tuum was bathed. It was hard to get her out of the pool and into a clean tunic. Somehow, Lucius produced soft wool slippers and she twirled around with the first laughter I'd heard from her. Her beautiful eyes grew wide to see golden peaches and roast lamb at the evening meal. We ate together in my room. She insisted on peeling my peach, which she deftly did. I decided I was mistaken about her age. She was possibly as old as ten. Her small wiry frame only made her look younger.

When evening came, we went up on the roof to see the moon rise. It was full – perhaps an omen of good things to come. Tuum pointed to the North Star and then to me. She pointed to the Little Dipper and tapped herself. I believe she meant that she would always look to me for direction.

Finally, we went to my room. Lucius had lit a lamp. He had a blanket and pallet there for Tuum. I put the pallet alongside my bed and motioned for her to lie down. She shook her head and dragged the pallet to the doorway. She put it across the entrance and pulled the blanket around her, smiling at the softness from Weaver's loom. She meant to protect me from any intruder.

I was happy with her joy over the small things that I took for granted – good food, clean clothes, a warm blanket. I also realized that I had a true slave. She meant to care for me. Maybe my disturbing dreams would fade with her close by. I smiled to myself. I couldn't get out of my room without disturbing her. In a faint way, I was Tuum's prisoner.

Chapter VIII

T hough I had some difficulty with our roles of mistress and slave, Tuum had none whatsoever because she was young and freed from the merchant's demands. When I opened my eyes the next morning, Tuum was sitting cross-legged at my bed watching me. In front of her was a bowl and pitcher of water. A clean towel was folded in her lap. She was ready as any obedient slave to help me wash and dress for the day ahead.

"Why, Tuum, how nice of you."

"Oh, Bibi, I thought you would never wake up." She smiled up at me. "Here's warm water from the kitchen. Maybe it is cold now." She stood up. "I'll get another pitcher."

"It's fine . . . fine." I was puzzled. "Why do you call me Bibi? My name is Procula." Other servants always called me by my name.

Solemn, Tuum shook her head. "You are Bibi."

I didn't argue, but I asked Lucius about its meaning. He shrugged, "It is an Indies word. Obviously from her manner, it's a title of respect."

We puzzled over Tuum's background. Was it possible that she was the offspring of some port-side liaison between an Indies sailor and a Sicilian girl? Or a silk seller lingered too long at some brothel? Had her mother died? Was she cast away to become a street urchin? I could almost thank the rug merchant for Tuum's shelter, in spite of his harshness. I wanted to believe that Tuum and I were destined to be together. Although I didn't believe in Zia Terentia's goddess, I gave a special prayer and offering when I showed Tuum the Temple of Isis.

I appreciated Roma anew when I saw it through Tuum's awestruck eyes – like the shrine of Isis in northwest Rome or near Villa Fontana, the huge sanctuary of Cybele. She slowly circled the many statues that personified Health, Honor, Faith, Fortune, Concord and other abstract ideas. We stood in the great marble Temple of Mars Ultor that Caesar Augustus built. Tuum craned her neck and uttered a soft Ooh when she stared up at three tall columns and tiptoed around the semicircular apse.

But her favorite trip was to a library, and there were many in Roma. Some were connected to temples. The Temple of Apollo stood nearby on the Palatine – so impressive with its fine sculptures by Myron and Scopas. It also contained a library and an art gallery. We pretended we were in Athens for an afternoon. I liked the libraries, too, because I could hear discussions and arguments about many topics – philosophy, Senate actions, the latest poetry and gossip. Sometimes, we also used a library located at a Palatine public bath. There were almost two hundred baths in Roma.

I lost track of the many times we borrowed AEsop's Fables. Perhaps Tuum was fascinated because AEsop had been a Phrygian slave of Iadmon, a Greek. Her favorite story was of the Ant and the Grasshopper. I think she saw herself as little and insignificant as an ant, but very clever.

How many times did I read it to her? One day I deliberately made a mistake. She caught me.

"No, Bibi," she pointed to the word grasshopper, "you said garden snake."

"How do you know?"

She blurted out. "Because I can read it!" Then, she covered her mouth in fear. Usually, slaves weren't allowed to read.

I tested her some more. Finally, she read the whole fable. When I praised her, she wanted to read other stories to me. From that time, I allowed her to pick out other books. We spent many happy afternoons comparing our choices.

Each day was a new adventure with Tuum. The other slaves were amused by her curiosity. She helped the gardener pluck off withered blossoms. She would shake a small rug with enthusiastic vigor. Often, she massaged my back and brought cool cloths for my headaches. I think she would have fought a lion in the amphitheater for me.

PROCULA | Marion H. Youngquist

In one very special way, I was indebted to her. From the time I arrived at Villa Fontana, Zia Terentia had wanted me to shine at something—anything. A talent would add to my value when arranging for my marriage.

At her dinner parties, Zia Terentia always presented some entertainment. Maybe a magician, or fortune-teller – who only predicted wonderful things for the guests – or musicians.

After one pleasant evening – the roast pheasant was especially good – a flute ensemble played. It was a family group--a musician with his five sons – ranging in age from fifteen to eight. They wore green caps with matching capes and played merry tunes. The father had a double flute, shaped like a V. It produced a lovely tone.

That night I made a mistake and told my aunt how much I enjoyed the music. "Oh, Zia, that family plays so beautifully, I hope they'll come again."

My aunt's eyes gleamed at my remark. "Procula! The flute's the answer! You must take music lessons!"

"I'm to play a double flute?"

"Any flute. Lucius can contact the Flute Master immediately. You will begin this week."

I suppressed a laugh. "I didn't mean . . ."

Zia Terentia didn't want any objections. "It may be the very thing to bring you out! You tuck yourself away reading too much. How will any young man notice you if you hide yourself under an orange tree with some long scroll?" She didn't wait for an answer. "Really, I think you'd be happiest if you lived in a library."

The Flute Master arrived the following week with exercises, a great deal of patience, and a new instrument for me. I really tried to play that simple tube with holes, but my heart wasn't in it. I would ask him to show me again – and again. Finally, his time would end, and he would gladly hurry away. I did practice alone and struggled with breath control. It was so easy to tell Zia Terentia that I would practice out in the garden. I would play a few notes and then pull a scroll from my sleeve and read – especially if Zia Terentia left for the baths.

Sometimes the Flute Master didn't come for several weeks with the excuse that his schedule was filled. Lessons were skipped during the summer when we were at Villa Forunata. Both he and I found excuses why I wasn't ready for a solo performance at a dinner party. Once I did join his sons and played a few notes that ended each phrase. Zia Terentia beamed at her friends about my talent. They listened and responded politely that Ilooked so regal and beautiful in my pale-yellow gown. They graciously didn't comment on my performance. My aunt was satisfied with her efforts, but I felt I was on an auction block, being marketed with extra value as a possible bride.

When Tuum joined the household, she was fascinated by the Flute Master. She studied his fingers with her quick eyes. Once I passed my flute to her. She hesitated.

"Show Tuum how to finger," I motioned to the Flute Master.

He sat down and worked with her as thoughtfully as with his own son. Soon Zia Terentia heard many more flute notes from the garden during my practice hour, but it was Tuum fingering the instrument while I read from a new edition of Ovid.

As the months passed, Tuum and I lived more within our own world while my aunt enjoyed her friends – afternoons of gossip, eating and games. I might play my flute nearby with lots of sour notes until I was asked to go elsewhere. My uncle escaped to his bank or Villa Mirabele. Always focused on money, he made shrewd decisions and formed a shipping partnership with some Greeks. He complained that Roma was too dependent on foreign territories – like Judaea – for grain to feed the poor. He worried when a ship was overdue. Piracy on the great Mare Internum was still a threat to cargo from distant and exotic ports, although the empire's navy had curbed much of it.

Tuum and I stayed to ourselves. She had a sunny personality. Often, we amused ourselves with imitations of Zia Terentia and her guests. I'd walk down the garden path with my nose in the air and eyebrows raised. Tuum would follow me with little mincing   steps, her head bowed as a humble slave.

Once Zia Terentia caught our charade. "Whatever are you doing?"

Afraid of what she would say, I shrugged, "I'm practicing being a lady of great importance!"

Zia Terentia thought I was serious. "Well, you certainly can never pass with that stiff walk. Watch me." She demonstrated a more relaxed movement and a faint nod. "Your problem, Procula, is that you don't feel superior to everyone else. You must cultivate . . . must feel . . . that innate excellence that is a mark of our family." She sighed, "You'll never learn. Superior people are born, not made."

Tuum and I suppressed our giggles as we watched her hurry away.

"Zio Ammonius is even worse," I whispered. "He struts like a peacock. He has a head like a donkey . . . and his brains are as little as a grasshopper's!"

I glanced around, afraid that I might be overheard. Tuum put her hand over her mouth, amused at my outburst. I felt a surge of defiant power with my remarks. My tongue would be my weapon if my life became more difficult. I practiced rolling my eyes and saying "Real-l-ly?" or "You're so-o-o right!" in a cynical tone. Soon I might shrug my shoulders and walk away from Zia Terentia with a snide "I real-l-ly don't care."

PROCULA | Marion H. Youngquist

When Julius married Iris, daughter of another banker, my aunt and uncle held a reception at Domum Fontana. The following afternoon Tuum and I recreated the party with a pantomime, mocking the affair. We pretended to be tipsy. We exaggerated greeting guests. We fawned over the floral arrangements. We laughed until we cried when Tuum pretended to be Iris – flitting among the guests with a high-pitched voice and nervous giggles.

At times like that, I became a child again for a few moments. Then, something would remind me that my childhood was over and soon I would be married, too.

It was at Julius' wedding that I first heard the name Pontius Pilate. His wife, Drusilla, was a guest – a beautiful red-head with arched eyebrows that gave her face   a skeptical look. She was a bit loud and flirted shamelessly, even with Zia Ammonius.

When I asked about her the next day, Zia Terentia said disdainfully, "Her husband is stationed with the troops in Gaul. Yet, the Senate has not allowed wives to join their husbands on foreign duty. Her affairs began the minute Pilate left Roma. I predict that he'll divorce her when he returns someday. Maybe he married her because she was distantly related to Senator Corvini . . . such an old and distinguished family. Or she married Pilate because he would be gone most of the time."

"Oh, no!" My face revealed shock and surprise.

"Don't look like that!" Zia Terentia laughed. "Do you think marriage means love and happiness? Be practical, Procula. Marriage is meant to preserve the family estate."

I didn't want to hear my aunt's viewpoint. Nevertheless, Zia Terentia – in her firm manner – began training me to supervise a household. She asked me to check the cleanliness of the library and several supply rooms.

"See that the corners and ceilings are thoroughly swept. No cobwebs! Spiders and mites can't live where things are clean. You have my permission to order the slaves to repeat their chores. If they're not to my standard, make them do them over. Otherwise, they get a light beating with only a switch . . . administered by the overseer."

She must have seen me grimace, as she continued. "No, soft excuses! It is a matter of cleanliness and health for Everyone. You must be firm. A switch is a warning. It is only after three hard beatings that we sell a slave. Our slaves are so well trained, we never sell them!"

"Tuum and I will check on the rooms," I mumbled while Tuum stood behind me.

"And don't let Tuum do any sweeping. She is your personal slave. She is above that work!" Zia Terentia waved us away. In Zia Terentia's world, everyone had a place, but she determined the order and status of each person.

Chapter IX

Zia Terentia seemed to soften toward me when I turned fifteen in late spring. Soon Octavianus returned from Pompeii, finished with his formal education. I seldom saw him. He relaxed at the seaside villa or cheered gladiator fights in the amphitheater where the loser was sacrificed when the crowd gave a thumbs down signal.

Whenever Octavianus stayed at Domum Fontana, I noticed he especially flattered Zia Terentia – no doubt to gain her support for his schemes. He was like many wealthy young Romans who were too lazy to work and bored with themselves. Money was assured for their future. Why worry about a career?

Nevertheless, when his mother's friends asked what he intended to do, Octavianus would vaguely answer Architecture--or Engineering. No one suggested that he join the banking firm. Was Zio Ammonius embarrassed over his son's gambling habit? Just before we left for the farm, Octavianus arrived from the Villa Mirabele. He was concerned about the months ahead. He stopped Tuum and me on the stairway to ask a favor.

"Procula, my mater values your opinion . . ."

I stifled laughter at that flattery. What did he want from me?

". . . I want to travel to Greece with my friends. But I need a reason to go. I've told my parents that I wish to study architecture . . . and where else, but among the magnificent buildings there? I need your support. Tell them that we've discussed it. . . and that you think it is an excellent idea for my future work."

"You and I scarcely speak. How can I lie like that?"

Octavianus pouted. "You're the silent one. You're still mad because I forgot about your little loan to me." He shrugged, "May I apologize?"

"You apologize?" I scoffed. "Are your fingers crossed behind your back? Don't ask me for any favor! Not one!"

Ex nihilo nihil– nothing comes from nothing.

"So, I made a mistake? Don't be so snippy! You can forgive one little mistake."

I was silent. I didn't want to add up all of my loans to him.

"Maybe I'll be an engineer and join the army . . . build roads and fine bridges. But first . . . can't I have some fun? Support me," he begged. At my silence, he sneered, "So you won't help? You are so-o-o perfect!" He stomped off to his room to change his toga before he left for the stadium.

Tuum stared down into the atrium if she were preoccupied with confused and troubling thoughts. Her hand rubbed the bannister with a nervous movement.

I asked her, "Tuum – what is the matter?"

"Please. . . always keep me. . . no matter what happens." She gave me an intense look. "When you marry with your own house, don't send me away."

"Of course not! Now go to the kitchen. Get us something cool to drink. I'll meet you in the garden. We'll read on this hot afternoon."

I went back to my suite which was my mother's old rooms. After I acquired Tuum, Zia Terentia admitted that I needed more space. Perhaps it also showed that she accepted my presence in the household. As I picked up our scrolls, I noticed something sparkled at the edge of Tuum's pallet. I lifted the corner and there were two coins, as if they'd been hidden there. I picked up the coins, puzzled over them. Had I dropped them?

I counted the money in my own coin pyx. How much I had placed there? I thought I was short some sesterces, but I couldn't be sure. Would Tuum really steal from me? She had grown distant in the past two weeks. Was it guilt? Or did she plan to run away?

In the garden, I observed her with quick glances while I read. I couldn't believe that she was a thief. Yet – that temptation was always in the household. Zia Terentia ruled that slaves must be sold if they were caught stealing. I didn't want to lose Tuum. In her time with me, she had provided loving companionship along with her sunny disposition. Although we didn't know her age or birthday, Lucius believed she was only two years younger than me. Now she reached my shoulder height. But none of that mattered if Zia Terentia found Tuum couldn't be trusted.

I acted quickly to reach the truth. I placed temptation clearly before her. The next afternoon, I sent Tuum ahead of me into the garden again. Then I emptied my money pyx and left some coins randomly on the table. I returned to the garden.

After a half hour, I said to Tuum, "I need my fan. Will you get it, please?"

She quickly returned with it. Shortly, I excused myself. When I walked into my room, I saw that the table was emptied of any money. I lifted her pallet and there were five small coins shoved under it. I closed my eyes, sick over her thievery, and sank down on my bed. I buried my head in my hands.

When I didn't return, Tuum came looking for me. I stared sternly at her. "Tuum, I'm very upset. I don't know what to do. My money was on the table when I sent you here for my fan. Now, all of it is gone!"

Her black eyes widened in fear. "No, Bibi! No! I didn't take it!"

"Then where is it?" I pulled back her pallet. "Look! My coins are right there! Where's the rest?"

"I can't tell you . . ."

I snapped angrily, "Don't lie!" and raised my hand and slapped her cheek so hard that my hand burned.

Tuum crumpled at my feet and grabbed my legs, crying, "Bibi . . . beat me. Hit me. I'll return the money, but don't send me away." She bent over ready for a whipping. I lifted my hand again, but then dropped it at my side. I trembled with disappointment.

"Get out!" I thundered. "I don't want to see you again."

Tuum ran from the room. I fell weeping on my bed. My faithful slave would be gone by morning when Zia Terentia found out. No doubt a servant in the hall had heard our exchange. It would spread over the household within an hour.

Shortly, there was a knock at the door.

I called out, "Go away!"

Instead, Lucius walked in and studied me a moment. "Procula, Tuum came to me, weeping that she must leave. You've accused her of stealing."

"Yes, I put her to the test. My money is gone. It's not the first time. Yesterday, I discovered some coins under her pallet. I've never counted it that closely, but I believe she's taken money on other days."

". . . But only recently? Within the last two weeks?" Lucius waited.

Silence. It hit me! Octavianus was the thief!

"But the coins under Tuum's pallet . . .?"

"A clever thief arranges for someone else to be blamed for his crime."

"Oh, Lucius, how can Tuum ever forgive me?" I buried my head in my hands again.

"The question is. . . how can you forgive yourself?" He turned at the door. "I'll send her back to you."

When Tuum came, I knelt and hugged her legs as she had done to me. "Forgive me," I begged. "I know you didn't steal. Don't ever leave me."

Tuum stroked my hair, "Bibi, don't cry. I knew you didn't mean to hit me."

That night Tuum put her pallet next to my bed. I reached down to hold her hand in mine. My hand still smarted from the slap I'd given her. I couldn't rub away the stinging. Humbled, I felt my burning palm for many weeks.

I confronted Octavianus and he didn't deny he'd borrowed my money again.

"It's your fault for leaving money on a table," he said, blaming me. "However, it was lucky money. I win when I bet. So, here's your share." He counted out my loss and added a couple of coins to soothe my anger. He shrugged and walked away.

"Just stay out of my room," I snapped. Why argue morality with him?

Tuum was watching from our doorway with a somber concerned face. I wanted to do something to lighten her mood and restore our easy relationship. I took off my gold bracelet and put it over her hand. I knew she thought it was the most beautiful piece that I owned.

"Here, I want you to have it."

She shook her head, "No, Bibi, I am only a slave."

"You are more to me than a slave. You are my friend, too."

Silently, Tuum handed the gold circle back to me.

"What can I do?" I asked. "I want you to have something precious."

". . . Only keep me . . . Forever."

"Forever! Nothing can separate us. I promise." I held up my hand as if I were taking an oath. Still Tuum didn't smile. I felt there was some wrong--much deeper than yesterday's mistake. I tried to coax a smile. "Let's go to the garden. You can read an old fable to me."

Usually, Tuum would respond by rolling her eyes and saying, "I'm too old for that!"

Instead, she was listless. She shrugged her shoulders and said, "If it pleases you . . ."

"Oh, Tuum, what is the matter? I was only teasing."

Suddenly, she grabbed my arm. "Oh, Bibi, don't sell me. Don't send me away."

"Whatever are you talking about?"

"I . . . I heard things . . . from the kitchen slaves."

Secrets were impossible. There was no privacy in Domum Fontana. Servants were always around – silently cleaning and caring for the family. They overheard conversations and decisions. They were beaten if they revealed any family secret, but no slave ever admitted knowing anything.

I paused, afraid of what she might tell me. "What did they say?"

". . . That you are soon to be married! Your new husband will sell me."

Those dreaded words! I knew sometimes I would hear them. When I reached sixteen, my future had to be settled. But now? To whom?

Carefully, I asked, "Did they tell you more?"

". . . Only that you know him well."

I thought hard. There was Domitius, a ship owner's son, who was shorter than I, and spent much time at the Circus. Once married, he wouldn't care where I went. Maybe we wouldn't live together very long before he would divorce me.

Then there was Valerius. His parents owned a country place next to Zia Terentia's estate. That would please her, as I might extend her land holdings through my marriage. He was nice-looking, too. This possibility excited me – just a tiny bit.

Or Publius – another banker's son. He was much like Julius – an eye for the ladies and a thirst for fine wine. He would give any wife a headache. I saw a sad future. Was I to become another Zia Terentia running to various shrines for answers and solace?

Like Tuum, I, too, grew morose. And waited.

Chapter X

It was true. The servants had overheard things correctly. Two nights later, Zio Ammonius called me into his library. Lucius was standing close by and studied a document carefully – no doubt a contract of marriage. For a moment his eyes met mine. My hands were clammy. I could scarcely breathe.

Zio Ammonius cleared his throat. "Procula, I have made a decision about your future. Your Zia Terentia has accepted the arrangement. You will marry your cousin Octavianus in the spring. You must sign this document." He pushed a parchment at me.

I stared at him, speechless. Slowly, I asked in a small voice, "Does Octavianus want to marry me?"

Zio Ammonius raised his eyebrows. "Of course! He knows that this is a good arrangement for everyone. Your care will stay within our family." He really meant that my fortune would stay within the family. "You will always have our protection. You will continue to live here. You have learned some things well from your aunt's example. Someday, you will supervise Villa Mirabele. You must apply yourself during these next months in preparation for your marriage. It will take place when the signs indicate that the time is right. That is all." He held out the scroll. "Lucius will sign this as a witness."

Lucius had said nothing during the conversation.

"Oh, THANK YOU," I mumbled sarcastically. Slowly, I wrote my name.

Later, when Zio Ammonius went to the baths, I sneaked into his library. As I snapped every stylus he had in two pieces, Lucius came up behind me. He scooped up the broken pens.

"I will replace these," he said, sternly. "It won't help to fight your uncle. His word is law."

I fled the room in tears. Not even in marriage could I escape Domum Fontana.

I scarcely knew Octavianus even though we both lived at Domum Fontana. He stayed in school at Pompeii. When he came back, he pursued friends and entertainment. Tuum overheard how much he gambled. Whatever the event, he found a way to turn it into a game of chance. At Julius' wedding, Octavianus placed bets on how soon he'd become an uncle. I pushed away thoughts that my dowry, invested in Villa Mirabele, might be mortgaged someday to pay off Octavianus' debts.

He spent most of his time with other young men. I asked Tuum to find out if he flirted with any girl at the baths or social affairs. Often, servants passed gossip between the great villas. She kept her eyes downcast and reported that Octavianus liked athletic contests. She added that he wanted to become an officer in the emperor's elite Praetorian Guard. This surprised me as he seemed a most undisciplined young man. Guard duty meant that he'd often be away. Innocently, I missed Tuum's cues about his behavior.

There was no question – I must become a bride. My fortune was taxed until I was married. My role was to bear three children. Then I wouldn't be taxed or under the rule of my husband. Also, I could wear the special garment –*ius trium liberorium* –that noted my devotion to the family and the state through motherhood. Many Roman officials were concerned about the falling birthrate and the great influx of foreigners. Roma was a cosmopolitan city of a million people. The affairs of state were still in the hands of old and wealthy families. They needed heirs to continue.

I couldn't inherit any of my uncle or aunt's estate if I remained unmarried – not that any would ever come to me while their two sons lived. Now that Julius and Iris were married, Julius would eventually inherit Domum Fontana and half his mother's country estate. Certainly, he was meant to succeed Zio Ammonius in the great bank. Octavianus, as a second son, was of less importance. We would live at Villa Mirabele when Zio Ammonius was tired of it or died.

Laws governed marriage and adultery. People – especially men – married to obey the law. Some loopholes allowed men to divorce their wives quickly. Family men were given preference in government appointments. At times, children were conveniently adopted and soon sent away.

What would become of me when I married Octavianus? In the morning after my uncle's announcement, Tuum and I met with Lucius in the garden. She stood behind the bench and massaged my shoulders as I poured out my heart to him.

"I don't want to marry Octavianus! Can't you do something? Send me away!" I shuddered thinking of my repulsive cousin. "He will grow mean if he joins the strict Praetorian Guard." I drew deep breaths to fight back tears.

Lucius chose his words carefully. "I doubt if Sejanus, the Prefect of the Guard, will accept him. Octavianus will need some army experience before he ever serves in Roma. Perhaps he can be appointed to serve as an officer in a province."

I brightened. That meant that my future husband would be far away.

"Can't we wait and marry after he returns?"

Lucius looked away. "No. Your uncle has already consulted the priests. It will be next spring. However, Octavianus will stay for several months in Greece with his friends. Don't despair, Procula. You will always have Tuum and Weaver and myself to help you."

Chapter XI

In the following months, Octavianus traveled while Zia Terentia instructed me in more household duties. Since I was already a member of Villa Fontana, I'd completed the custom of a betrothed girl living with her future family for a year. I ordered meals, linens, flower arrangements, and checked furniture repairs with Lucius' help. I studied the Cook's preparations and didn't report the extra portions he prepared when there was a banquet. The kitchen staff enjoyed feasting too, although by law they were granted only simple fare. However, I kept a close watch on pantry supplies. Cook respected my orders. That year passed with many sighs from Zia Terentia. Octavianus returned heavier without change. Someday he'd be jowly like his mother.

When it came time to marry, we observed the appropriate customs. We went through the old Roman betrothal rite of breaking a straw. I snapped my end quickly and drew the larger piece – meaning that I would have more authority than my future husband. There was some laughter among the crowd. Octavianus frowned and sulked a bit until he went to the garden with his friends for their dice games.

We married in June, an auspicious time because the birds were flying – another proper observance. All the rituals were observed. My hair was braided in six sections in an upswept coronet. Zia Terentia had a special ornament made – a thin glass globe crown, encrusted with pearls – to cap my hair. Weaver created a lovely scarlet hood to wear with my golden stola shot with flame-colored threads. The traditional cord around my waist was knotted. I carried a bouquet that I had picked myself – roses surrounded by sprigs of fresh rosemary and lavender. Frequently, I lifted it to enjoy the aroma. So, I managed to hold back my tears.

When I put my right hand in Octavianus', the guests shouted *Felicitas*. Our banquet lasted all day with roast pigeons and lamb with mint jelly. We offered a seed cake to the proper god, Jupiter Farreus, and shared a piece with each other. The festivities were as lavish as if I had been a daughter instead of a niece. My life now belonged to Octavianus. Perhaps my dowry paid for our wedding expenses.

We paid homage to each household spirit – Vesta for hearth and home, Penates for the household store – that it be plentiful, and Genius for the power to continue the family. We were given a small Genius to take with us to our future home. It was in a cedar box and handed to Octavianus to carry. I turned away when I saw him accept it. The last thing I wanted were several littler gamblers to manage. Anyway, I was a Stoic – I didn't believe in household spirits. Secretly, I doubted that even the spirit of a dead Caesar Augustus' could do much anymore for the Roman empire. People were unhappy with the rule of Tiberius, a tight-lipped and rather remote emperor.

Was it at Lucius' suggestion that Octavianus and I should begin our wedded life at Zia Terentia's estate? We left after the banquet--Tuum and I, Octavianus and his servant – for the farm. The wine had gone to his head. He was snoring loudly when we arrived. He did not carry me across the threshold because I hurried ahead. Tuum followed closely behind me. I also avoided being smeared with oil and fat. Nor did I tie a thread of wool on the doorposts. When I didn't give birth within a year, the servants whispered that my failure occurred because these customs hadn't been observed.

The steward's wife led us to the bridal chamber. I couldn't look at my new husband. No doubt the steward's wife thought I was shy. She winked at me as Octavianus entered, his left arm draped over his slave's shoulder for support. I knew Tuum would be outside our door, ready with another glass of wine or a sleeping potion for Octavianus if he tried to beat me.

Everyone left. We were alone. Octavianus yawned and looked at the bed, covered in the finest white linen which had been perfumed with lavender and rose petals. A vase of orange blossoms added a lovely sent to the room. Oil lamps cast a soft radiance. Everything was ready for a romantic night – except the two of us. My hands were ice-cold with fear.

Octavianus pulled a pair of dice – no doubt, weighted – from his sleeve. "I challenge you . . . two out of three rolls . . . for the bed." Perhaps I stared at him, because he added, "You don't think I'll sleep with you, do you?"

I shrugged, trying to be very casual, unconcerned. "I didn't beg to marry you. You can have the bed."

"No, I want to play for it!" He grew louder. "If I want to play a game, you must play! A wife obeys her husband!" he yelled, weaving slightly toward me.

"I never gamble!"

"I said . . . PLAY! NOW!"

Only a few hours had passed, and we fought like an old married couple. The servants listening outside must have been doubled over with laughter.

Octavianus grabbed a lamp-stand with his right hand. "You'll do as I say!"

Frantically, I looked around the room. There was no place to hide, but I moved quickly behind a three legged stand. It held a bowl of red apples.

"Never!" I yelled.

Octavianus started toward me. If I were cornered, I could expect a gash on my head, or worse. Octavianus was strong with the heaviness of Zia Terentia. His face was red with anger. As he rushed forward, I backed into a wall. Suddenly his foot caught on the table leg. He fell, cursing Zeus, Neptune, Apollo and any deity he could recall in his drunken state. He lay there, the table tumbled over his legs and apples all around him. The broken bowl had cut his hand.

I called Tuum and Octavianus' slave. My new husband was bandaged and helped into bed. Tuum gave him a sleeping potion. He quieted down.

Tuum opened a tall cabinet. Inside were extra blankets and a goose down pallet. She pulled it out and placed it at the far side of the room with two blue blankets on top.

"Bibi, I'll stay here if you need me."

I shook my head. Tuum shut the door and left me with my sleeping mate.

I looked at him – the opposite of an ideal husband, according to Roman culture. It was expected that a man would provide the dwelling place – actual wood and stones – for a home. The wife would nurture him and the family with food and companionship. Together, they would build adomus –a spiritual abode where they could retreat from the world when they stepped across the threshold. I knew that Octavianus and I could never create that sacred space. Lucius, Tuum and everyone else – except his parents and myself – knew that Octavianus wanted to live and move only in a male world. In my marriage, I would not be stuck with a demanding husband in bed. Whether I could ever have a life apart from my uncle and aunt might be a different challenge.

I snuffed out the oil lamp and burrowed down, cushioned by soft feathers. I thought about the wedding festivities. Certainly, the banquet was lavish. I laughed aloud at Tuum's prank. She had captured some spiders and dropped them in the dark wine cups. As Zio Ammonius started his welcome, he saw a spider floating in his wine. He put down his cup and asked for another. That, too, had a spider. He studied it a moment and flicked it out with his finger. Glaring at Zia Terentia, he gave a brief speech and the ceremony began.

People praised me, as a beautiful bride. I was pleased that I had played my part well. I was lulled to sleep by the snores of my new husband.

In three days, Octavianus left me for business in Genua. I knew that he needed to gamble while he waited for his army assignment. A month later, an officer's commission came through. True to Lucius' prediction or arrangement, he was stationed far away in Gaul – one of five thousand men in a legion, commanded by a chief captain, tribunicius Pontius Pilate. It was the second time that I had heard that name.

Chapter XII

Tuum and I were familiar with Villa Fortunata. We always spent summers there with Zia Terentia during Roma's hot weather. The farm was a self-sustaining community. It also provided Domum Fontana as well with olive oil, wool, wine, meat, cheese and wood throughout the year. Now that I was a married woman, wife of the second son, I had a new status and respect. I was the household authority if Zia Terentia was not in residence.

When either Gaius, the steward, or his wife came to me for a decision, I would ask "What do you think?" Usually, I accepted their suggestion. In this way I posed no threat to the smooth pattern that they had established. Gradually, they came with more concerns – like a fight between two stable hands. I could have ordered the lads beaten and sold.

One, a lanky fellow older than I, stood with his cap in hand, afraid to look at me. The other lad, younger with a set jaw and fiery eyes, was the accuser. "He stole my lucky charm. It's a furry paw with a leather thong. He has it hidden in his tunic!"

I held out my hand. The culprit dropped the prized possession into my hand. I picked it up and studied it carefully. The younger slave wanted to grab it. I looked at both of them smiling. "Yes, I can see this is a fine charm, but it will only bring luck to its owner."

I saw some anger leave the younger face. The older boy trembled, afraid that I would order severe punishment.

Instead, I said, "If you like this so much, ask your friend . . ." (I emphasized the word) ". . . how he came by it. He'll help you get your very own charm . . . one that will work just for you."

Both thought slowly about what I said and then nodded.

"Shake hands," I commanded, ". . . and be about your work. You can hunt for the right animal tonight when you finish your chores. Go hunting together. Four eyes are better than two."

They left not saying much, but two days later the tall boy proudly showed me a skunk tail (still smelling) that was his power to ward off evil spirits. Quickly, I had him light incense in thanksgiving to one of Zia Terentia's goddesses. I sent the youth back to the stable as quickly as possible. Then I filled vases with lavender to restore a sweet scent to the room.

Zia Terentia arrived each summer for three years, during Roma's hottest weather. Occasionally Lucius came and checked reports that Aulus, the overseer, sent to him. Tuum and I were accepted and appreciated on the estate for our own qualities. Tuum helped the midwife when a new baby was born. I had the power to sell slaves and discipline them. I kept families together, so while I was there, no workers were sold. People trusted me.

Aulus was upset that old Mamaea was too feeble to work any longer. She had been kept for many years, even in limited health because she knew herbal secrets. She was childless and refused to pass on her knowledge to anyone else. Aulus was so angry that he wanted to free her and let her die as a ward of the state. This often happened to old slaves.

One morning Tuum and I went to the dark shed where Mamaea lay on a dirty straw pallet. No doubt Aulus had hoped to make her beg for fresh straw though he was not a mean overseer. He meant to bargain with her to teach some younger slave her secrets. Mamaea knew who I was and mouthed a toothless greeting. She bowed her head in deference to my position as the head of the household.

I kneeled beside her and smoothed her brow with my hand. "Tuum, sponge Mamaea's forehead. She seems feverish." I bent low over her. "What do you need? How may we help you?"

That simple act brought her response. She lifted her head slightly and whispered in a raspy tone, "I need some tea . . . some mint tea. Go to the far pasture. Lemon mint is there. Bring two handfuls and wash it with well water. You must steep it in boiling water while you clap your hands gently fifteen times." She lay back on the bed, exhausted from giving directions. "Bring it to me before sundown." Then she closed her eyes.

PROCULA | Marion H. Youngquist

I sat with her while Tuum followed her instructions. The tea did revive her, and I ordered that she be fed a nourishing soup and fresh bread for a sop. When Tuum and I returned the next day, Mamaea was more alert and readier to sit up. At the same time, I ordered not only fresh straw, but a goose down pillow. Other slave women came by to see the luxury granted to Mamaea.

One day, Tuum and I came with a stylus and a wooden tablet. I asked Mamaea what I would need if I developed a cough. She whispered in my ear where the horehound plant could be found and how to mix a horehound syrup with honey. Gradually, she revealed other cures. She shook her head angrily that the excreta of dogs should ever be used for heart pain when a digitalis plant was more effective. And dandelion wine – the leaves should be picked during the full moon – was a cure for many things.

As I made notes, Tuum would sketch the plants. In this way, we put together a household guide for illness. Mamaea seemed eager to share her knowledge, since it was being written down in a book which she could never read, but would be her legacy nevertheless.

My interest in her was beneficial for other slaves, too. I realized how damp and cold the dirt floors were in the slave area. I remembered the imperfect tiles that were often discarded in Arretium. I arranged for a large shipment. When it arrived, the slave quarters were tiled during the second winter. Some were decorated squares. Many were colorful. The mixture made for a patchwork floor – smooth and clean. The tile floors set a new standard for a rural area. Our slaves were proud to work under better conditions and envied by other farm workers. I became known as a good domina – mistress of the slaves.

Country life had a special rhythm, guided by the seasons and crops. In spring, the goddess Ceres was honored with offerings of wheat, barley, beans and mustard. A thanksgiving rite to Janus was celebrated with wine and incense at the fall harvest. We paid homage to Mars Silanus in the woodland for the safety of oxen. I sent offerings of meal, lard, meat and wine by the two stable-hands, as women were not granted favors by the god. There was a celebration when the pear trees blossomed. I chose a pig for a sacrifice by the woodcutters. It seemed that the slightest pretext was a reason to stop farm work and celebrate.

I missed Roma and the libraries. Lucius sent books and kept us informed about current events. He wrote that Tiberius had conscripted some Jews for the dangerous work of policing the Isle of Sardinia – which meant almost certain death. He had expelled other Jews from Roma. I remembered the Jewish merchants, west of the Tiber River. Some were quaint peddlers with interesting wares when they came to Domum Fontana. Now, their schools and synagogues would be gone. Roma would be less colorful.

They would be missed. I knew I would never live in Roma again as long as Octavianus served in Gaul. I preferred the country, especially if it meant that my absent husband remained far away.

One day a coach clattered into the farm courtyard. Zio Ammonius stepped out, obviously upset. A gray sky added to his somber mood.

"Procula, you must return to Roma at once. Your Zia Terentia has suffered a stroke. She is paralyzed. I need your help. Lucius can't run the household by himself."

Was this true? Lucius, for many years, had run Domum Fontana with wise and capable shrewdness. Did Zia Terentia really want me? Once, she had hoped for a brilliant union with a prominent family for her favorite son. That was another odd quirk at Domum Fontana. Zia Terentia claimed that Zio Ammonius loved Julius best – as the eldest being groomed to run the bank. Her own true-heart belonged to Octavianus as he looked like her own father. It was a divided house in every way – even by sons.

I knew that Zia Terentia would demand much care. Her imperial manner kept any servant from very deep devotion. She changed her personal attendant almost as often as she changed her hairstyle.

"She's begging for you." I saw the pleading in Zio Ammonius' eyes.

"She wants me to be another slave. Forget it!" I turned away.

"If you would only understand . . . "He paused. "I'll try to make up for our past differences."

I was sarcastic. "Only differences? My marriage was only a difference of opinion? I like my life here!" I walked out and left him standing there. I heard his carriage leave.

Before mid-afternoon, Lucius arrived with the same message – I was needed at Domum Fontana. This time I listened to him.

"Procula, you must come. I cannot run the household and supervise your aunt's care, too. Daily, she grows more frustrated and difficult. Please. . . come for my sake."

How could I refuse? Lucius had been my friend and protector during my early years. I knew I must help him. Although my resentment over my forced marriage had grown deeper through the years, I would deal with Zio Ammonius later. I ordered Tuum to pack our trunks.

Before we left the farm, the slaves and freedmen lined up to wave us goodbye. The two young stable-hands thrust gifts at me. The tall one had created a special charm from a raccoon's foot on a new leather thong. Proudly, he hung it around my neck. The other lad had three feathers and a sprig of rosemary tied together. I tucked it into my sash and he, too, smiled, with tears in his eyes. The cook brought an extra loaf of his mixed-grains bread and whispered, ". . . Just for you."

As the coach pulled away, both Tuum and I felt a sadness. Lucius sat tense and quiet, deep in thought. It was almost like the trip from Arretium nine years ago, except this time I would arrive in Roma as a daughter-in-law. That should make a difference.

Chapter XIII

My status was apparent as soon as I entered. The servants lined up to greet me. Perhaps I looked older, more mature. I moved with a certain authority after supervising the farm household. Zio Ammonius was not there.

"Please, Procula, your Zia Terentia is anxious for you!" Lucius said.

Tuum and I followed him into Zia Terentia's suite. She was in a semi-darkened room, filled with statues and many vigil lamps. The mixture of scented oils was heady and overpowering. Statues of gods and goddesses covered every surface – Diana of the Ephesians, Pan, Juno, Chloe. She wanted help from all sources, but none offered comfort or solace.

As I bent over her, I saw how illness had ravaged her body. She turned her face away with difficulty, so I wouldn't see the half-closed eye, the mouth pulled down and drooling, her right arm limp at her side. I kissed her forehead, remembering how coldly she had greeted me when I came to Domum Fontana as a child.

"I'm here, Zia Terentia. I'll take care of you." Although I harbored resentment, I also felt pity for this once-proud matron of Villa Fontana.

Tears rolled down her cheeks. With great difficulty, she mumbled, "To think, I end like this."

That was the last thing I ever heard her say. In the night, Zia Terentia had another stroke that left her mute and partially blind. So, I became her constant attendant (or slave) which would have been impossible without the support of Tuum and Lucius. Zia Terentia wanted me to sit by her bed, hold her hand and soothe her forehead. If I left, she'd let out painful grunts until I returned and calmed her again.

Before my marriage, I wondered why my aunt agreed for me to be the wife of her favorite son. Along with my dowry, perhaps she realized that she could control me better than a wealthy senator's daughter. I took care of her country place. Now in illness, she still managed my life.

Sometimes when Zia Terentia slept, Tuum sat for a few hours in my place, so I could rest. Occasionally, I even slipped away to the public baths. We discovered Zia Terentia knew I had left because Tuum's hand didn't have a wedding ring. So, I had a companion ring made for Tuum and that helped calm Zia Terentia when I was away. I dabbed my sandalwood perfume on Tuum to add to our deception.

Octavianus did get special leave to see his mother. He came with another officer – a stocky florid man who studied me with some interest. Octavianus and I had a stilted private conversation in Zio's library. We both agreed we were looking well and taking care of our respective duties. He liked his work. He was on the support staff, keeping records, and was proud to be serving in Pontius Pilate's legion, although he was at an outpost and didn't see him. Octavianus was heavier. Evidently, his commander kept his troops well fed, as Gaul had excellent wines and produce.

Octavianus stayed for a week. He and his friend went to the Circus Maximus and enjoyed Roma's delights. It was difficult for him to see his invalid mother. No doubt, she would have been distressed to know he was there, but she seldom responded to anything. Octavianus held her hand, silent in thought.

His coach clattered into the entrance court. A few servants, Tuum and I gathered to say good-bye. Suddenly, Octavianus turned and hugged me – his face a quick mixture of regret and relief. His friend tapped him on the shoulder, they climbed in and were gone. It was the last time I would ever see my husband.

Zio Ammonius retreated to his seaside villa. It was obvious that he couldn't deal with either illness or approaching death. Both interfered with his Epicurean belief that life should be lived for pleasure.

Days went into weeks, and weeks into several months. Zia Terentia died after midnight the tenth day of Juno. Quickly, Zio Ammonius ordered a cremation. We properly dressed in black. We served meals during the nine funeral days when sheep were sacrificed daily. On the final day of mourning, the household donned white robes to celebrate a return to life. Zio

PROCULA | Marion H. Youngquist

Ammonius and his friends went off to the baths, while Tuum and I retreated to the garden. It was odd that I had inherited Zia Terentia's position so quickly. I was determined to be a good domina and not treat the servants in her haughty manner. In a strange way, I thought of myself as a survivor.

I assumed Zio Ammonius would still reside in his lavish seaside mansion. However, now that Zia Terentia was gone, he often stayed in the city. Lucius and I were always prepared when he appeared with extra dinner guests. Often, Julius and Iris came to join his parties. By now, they had two children and another on the way. Although I acted as hostess, Iris would arrive and overrule me. If I had roast boar on the menu, she would demand that pheasant be added. I would nod to the cooks that I understood. She even gave me advice.

"You should enjoy yourself a little," she slyly suggested. "Flirting isn't against the rule of marriage. Everyone needs a little adventure. You're such a prude."

I turned away. If I dreamed of love, I could never find a face for it. Since my return, my contacts had been limited because of Zia Terentia's illness. Now, Zio Ammonius – an eligible man – was invited out a great deal. Tuum even reported rumors that he was seeing a younger official's wife. During the summer months, he retreated to his seaside villa while Tuum and I returned to the country for six happy weeks.

In some ways, I supervised three households. I gained new respect for Zia Terentia during that year. It was not so simple making many decisions and directing the servants. Lucius was thorough and detailed in his records. I learned much from him about handling tradesmen and quarrels within the staff. And dear Tuum was always nearby to insist that I rest and relax and attend the public baths. One day I realized that I had an envied social position when I found myself surrounded by other young matrons eager for an invitation to Domum Fontana. It was still hard to believe that I belonged there.

At either Villa Fortunata or Domum Fontana, my days fell into a pattern of keeping the households running efficiently. I knew that I was necessary for Zio Ammonius to move easily between Roma and Villa Mirabele. I kept busy and thought of myself as a domestic engineer.

Nevertheless, after Zia Terentia's death, I grew reflective. My marriage was one of convenience much like hers. I was not free. Octavianus would live a long time, as Tiberius had decreed no more wars. The empire's borders were secure except for occasional uprisings. My childish dreams had ended long ago. Hope without substance was a fantasy. My future seemed to be days of endless routine.

Empta dolore docet experientia – Experience bought by pain teaches.

I waited.

Chapter XIV

Shortly before Saturnalia, Zio Ammonius returned from his office with an ashen face. Immediately, I knew that something was wrong. Lucius, standing near, wore a grave look. I followed them into the Library. Lucius closed the door and poured a glass of wine. He handed it to me.

"Procula, I have some very sad news," Zio Ammonius said. "An official courier arrived this morning. Octavianus died two weeks ago." He choked on the last words.

I stared, wondering if I had heard him correctly. What happened? A military skirmish on the border of Germanicus? A heroic act to save another soldier? Or was he killed in a quarrel over a gambling debt?

"Dead? But how?"

"The letter only said that he developed a terrible cough with chills and fever. He died, calling out for his mother."

I was stunned. I looked at both, and realized they wanted some kind of reaction from a grieving widow. I turned away, thinking of my money that Octavianus had stolen, the sneers under his breath about my reading, his gambling, his right to my dowry, and the sham of our marriage. Most of all, I thought about his wasted life – and I buried my head in my hands and cried honest tears. He had wasted my life, too.

Both Lucius and Zio Ammonius patted my shoulder. I regained my composure and left. Lucius said he would announce my husband's death. Tuum already knew and had black clothing ready.

Again, there was a repeat of nine days of mourning. But there was a difference this time. With Zia Terentia, I was a daughter-in-law – a lesser one for being married to the second son. Now I was a widow receiving condolences, almost twenty-three years old and not unattractive – at least according to Tuum as she brushed my hair and twisted it into a stylish knot on top. She secured it with a rope of jet-black beads.

"You are beautiful," Tuum said simply. "All the single men in Roma will be calling on you."

"Tuum . . . you have a fantasy that some foreign prince will whisk us away to Athens or Alexandria. That won't happen. I must run the household here."

Tuum was silent. I wondered – what had she overheard when the slaves whispered on the back stairs?

"Everyone wants you to stay, but they say that Julius and Iris will soon move in here," she admitted. "He is the eldest son and this house will belong to him, now that Octavianus is . . . is gone. Your Zio Ammonius will live in his seaside villa."

"His villa?" My voice was hard. "My dowry bought that property. I hope he drowns there someday." I was bitter. I didn't intend to forgive him – ever.

Octavianus' death had changed everything. Though we had no children, I was heir to his portion of the farm, and half of Domum Fontana. Someday, I would have his share of Villa Mirabele, although Zio Ammonius might remarry and have a second family. Could he dismiss my claim? My future seemed very uncertain.

Perhaps I could move into a house of my own. I asked Lucius about my dowry. "

Ask your uncle . . ." he stumbled, ". . . your . . . father-in-law. He has invested it. He has great ability with his banks and his ships and property . . . a real Midas' touch."

So I confronted Zio Ammonius late that afternoon. "Your dowry . . ." he hesitated, ". . . was invested wisely. An initial sum bought a partnership in a grain ship. . . a tidy profit there. That money helped complete the seaside villa. It was built for Octavianus and you someday . . . to stay within the family." He paused, "Then . . . if you must know, a portion bought Octavianus' position as an army clerk so he wouldn't bear arms. Money is power. The enlisting officer . . . through Sejanus . . . accepted his application along with a bribe. Money bought his officer's commission, too." He was silent a moment. "It wasn't too difficult since the Emperor is glad for Roman soldiers. Too many of our troops are foreign adventurers."

I mulled over all that Zio Ammonius had said. I realized that from the time we left Arretium years ago, he had planned my marriage to Octavianus – just as he had planned to keep my dowry within the family.

"Julius wants to move his family into Domum Fontana." He added, "Of course, you can stay here and assist Iris . . ."

I gave a bitter laugh. "Am I to be Iris' slave now? Do Julius and Iris expect me to be a nursemaid for their children? Iris would love to give me orders!" I added, sarcastically.

He frowned at my response. "If you won't stay here, there's always the country estate. I thought you enjoyed Villa Fortunata."

"That's a convenient way to get rid of me!"

"I didn't mean . . ."

"This time I'll decide what I want to do! You won't run my life again!"

I left Zio Ammonius standing there.

Somehow, the farm was in the past. My present was sliding away from me. I had no idea where I wanted to go in the future. If Zio Ammonius remarried, then where would I be? What if he decided to marry me? Such things happened in Roman society. I trembled at the thought. I really had no home at all.

I went to aloggia in the garden. Tuum played the flute while I mulled over our situation. I felt a terrible longing to belong somewhere as familiar as my childhood home in Arretium. It came to me. We would go back to my old home I would live in my father's house again!

Both Lucius and Zio Ammonius were cool about my plans. I wouldn't yield.

"Are you sure?" my uncle asked in a grave voice. "You've been gone so long."

Lucius added. "Things will be different." I knew he thought it was a foolish move.

"Stay the winter, if you must . . ." Zio Ammonius said, ". . . but return in springtime. I'll . . . we'll . . . all miss you."

I didn't believe him, but he believed me. He sent Lucius to Arretium to find a house for us. Lucius returned with news that my old home was occupied by two families who had migrated from Hispania to work in tile production.

Within two weeks, Tuum and I left in a carriage, with our trunks on top, and started northward to Arretium. We were in high spirits, because I could point out landmarks along the way. I prepared Tuum for the joys ahead with an elaborate description of my old home. How enjoyable life would be! I was sure the present owners would allow us to pick a few fresh plums from the tree beside our grape arbor.

"Oh, we will have a fine life in Arretium!" I promised Tuum.

As Zio Ammonius and Lucius surmised, things didn't work out as I had dreamed.

Our old cook and her husband had moved away. Lucius hired a freedman's daughter and son as servants. When I arrived, I found they quarreled over their duties. They didn't respect Tuum because she was a slave. They resented my instructions in Roma ways. Few potters recognized me as I had grown older. There were new foremen and a Greek director of the tile cooperative. Even the buildings looked different--not as large or impressive as I had remembered. My old home seemed so small. It had fallen into disrepair. A chicken coop had replaced the plum tree. Worst of all, the winter was cold and damp.

Tuum developed a hacking cough and high fever. One night she became delirious and cried out, "Bibi . . . I want to go home . . . I want to go home."

I realized, then, that I had done to Tuum what Zio Ammonius had done to me – taken her from the only home she knew. I made the decision that we would leave Arretium. My childhood had been gone for many years, and my old home was lost forever. I had to admit – my winter in Arretium had been an impulsive and headstrong move.

When spring came, I notified Zio Ammonius that I wanted to return to Roma. Could Lucius find a small house for Tuum and me? My uncle replied by return courier.

My dear Procula. . . Your suite is waiting as Julius and Iris live on the mons Capitolinus, near her friends. It will be good to have you here. I spend most of my time in Roma now. I hope that you will act as my hostess at Domum Fontana. Often, I entertain at small dinner parties. Both Lucius and I will appreciate your help."

I studied the letter, written on his finest parchment, and sealed with his ring. Was this very personal note an effort to smooth relations between us?

My answer was "Yes, I will return" – for the time being.

I left Tuum to pack our trunks while I walked to the cemetery where my parents were buried – now a changed landscape as the trees had grown taller. A new path wound through the woods. However, a huge flat stone remained at the tomb entrance. I went there for a last time to sit and meditate.

PROCULA | Marion H. Youngquist

I closed my eyes. I deeply inhaled the pungent aroma of nearby pines. I listened to a dove call to her mate. I felt the sun warm on my cheeks and remembered my sunny childhood. I bit into a wild strawberry – my tongue tasting a tart sweetness. I dug into the red clay, lifted the dirt to smell – to crush into my palm – to rub beneath my nails. I let some dry soil sift through my fingers. With this memory, I could always close my eyes and be in Arretium again. I sat there for an hour. Time stood still. Without looking back, I walked down the slope to whatever lay ahead.

Chapter XV

T uum was delighted to be back in Roma, and that made me happy. She assisted me in running the household. Lucius was now free to attend to the business affairs of both Domum Fontana and the country estate. Zio Ammonius and I were cordial, much like business partners – respectful, but not friendly. Our life resumed its old pattern.

One autumn morning, Zio Ammonius said, "Oh, did I mention that there will be several guests for dinner this evening? One will be Pontius Pilate. He offered his personal sympathy when we met at the baths yester-day. He is a chief captain, just returned from Gaul. He knew of Octavianus, mainly by reputation."

What kind of reputation did Octavianus have? I was determined not to appear as foolish as my dead husband may have been. I took extra care with my appearance. I dressed in a conservative way – in a soft dark blue wool stola, banded with a silver design and a wide silver belt. I wore no jewelry – only a thin silver chain around my wrist. It was simple and elegant, right for a widow after a year of mourning.

Tuum came into the room breathless and looked at me with approval. "You are the loveliest rose of all. Just pinch your cheeks for a touch of color." She patted my face.

"Thank you, Tuum. You always say the right thing." I smiled, amused by her effort to prepare me for Zio's party. "What about his guests?"

Her eyes danced with excitement. "Ah, a stranger. . . Pontius Pilate. . . just arrived. Wait until you meet him! He looks so strong and so-so . . ." She rolled her eyes with pleasure.

After a pause, I recalled his name. "Oh, I think he's married."

"No... no! His wife divorced him years ago." "

Then he must be old . . ." Intrigued, I sweetened my breath with drops of myrrh.

". . . Old enough! Maybe over forty. . . but not too old!"

Now I was curious. Tuum circled me, smoothed my gown across my shoulders and gave me a push toward the door. I slowly descended the stairs and entered the atrium. I nodded to the others. Pontius Pilate had his back to me. Then Zio Ammonius tapped him on the shoulder, drew me forward and introduced us.

Pilate turned. I saw his quick dark eyes, amused and bored, change to surprise. He murmured a low, "Ave! What have we here?"

". . . Only a housekeeper," I said, quietly, and moved toward Iris.

He followed me. "Not so fast!" he said, blocking my path. "You can't brush off a stranger. It's not polite. How have we missed knowing each other?"

"I'm here every day," I answered, a bit cynical. "I'm chained to Roma."

"I don't believe that," Pilate grinned. "But then, if you're interested in Gaul, I can . . ." He stopped, realizing that Octavianus had died there. "I'm sorry. I didn't mean to remind you of your sorrow."

I gave him a small smile. "Well, I'm something . . . of a . . . Stoic," I fumbled, trying to find the right words to put both of us at ease. "I hope Octavianus served the Emperor to the best . . . of his ability." Perhaps things that aren't said are more important than spoken words. I faced him fully. "I would really like to hear about Gaul sometime. I know that your soldiers enjoyed a very good cuisine. And very good wine!"

Pilate grinned, "I like a good table. An army marches on its stomach as well as its feet. I enforced discipline . . . and kept the morale high with good equipment and good food." His warm hand cradled my elbow to guide me to a bench beyond the fountain. He motioned for a glass of wine, which he handed to me with a slight flourish. As he leaned forward, I saw his temples were slightly gray. Tuum had guessed his age correctly. His ruddy complexion and erect military bearing gave him a distinguished look. He had a firm jaw and thoughtful dark eyes. He would not lose many arguments.

He lifted his glass. "To you, dear Procula. May your life ahead be filled with joy."

I nodded Gracia. "And may you, Pilate, find your days in Roma as pleasant as Gaul."

"I believe I will!"

We touched our glasses and sipped carefully. We were almost the same height. We were like two panthers stalking each other.

Pilate studied his wine. He sniffed the bouquet. "Very nice," he said, looking at me. "It matches the hostess with a certain elegance."

"From ours . . . Zio's . . . estate, north of here. Our winemaker has been there forever. This vintage is several years old. I spent several years at the farm after my marriage. I may have picked these grapes," I laughed, feeling more light-hearted with him there.

Zio Ammonius announced that dinner was ready, and again Pilate guided me. I didn't resist. The warmth of his touch was reassuring – a connectedness that had been missing all my life. I didn't sit near him during the meal, but our eyes met, and he would smile as if we shared a secret. We were deeply attracted to each other.

When he left that night, he said he would soon stop by. He wanted me to enjoy a bottle of Chablis from Gaul. And that is what he did – late the next afternoon while Zio Ammonius was still at the baths. Soon I expected Pilate to call. We sat in the garden on pleasant days. He told me about his travels, and I told him about my life – my childhood and how I came to Domum Fontana. I didn't reveal Zia Terentia's coolness, or Zio Ammonius' remoteness. Or my forced marriage. Pilate was intelligent enough to guess the truth.

One afternoon, Pilate simply took my hand and said, "Procula, we are a lot alike. You have no home, nor do I. Shortly, I'll get a new assignment. I expect to be made Governor of Syria. The present one is detained in Roma. I know Sejanus. . .," his jaw tightened with some memory, ". . . and he owes me a favor. I supported his appointment to command the Praetorian Guard. Since he directs the Emperor's affairs, I'm sure he will secure my position as well."

By now, I knew what he would ask. I shrugged, "Neither Sejanus nor the Emperor matter . . ."

"But they do . . . very much! However, I want us to marry now, so I can present you in Roma as the future queen of Syria!"

I laughed, "That's an impossible title for a Governor's wife."

"Then you will be my very own queen. Away with those who disagree!" He waved his hand dramatically, smiling broadly.

I didn't know Pilate well, but he appeared intelligent and honorable. He was right. We were alike – childless, homeless, without close family ties. My future seemed routine – Domum Fontana in the winter, and summer in the country. Forever, I would supervise my uncle's households. And where would I be if Zio Ammonius married again? Lucius hinted he might leave Roma to live elsewhere. Then, Tuum and I would really be alone.

I looked away, thinking of my wedding and Octavianus. "Pilate, my marriage was arranged . . ."

"I know that."

"I know nothing about love . . . or marriage."

Pilate took both of my hands in his and kissed them. "I know a great deal more about you, than you do about me. I'm willing to chance it. I need your love. Marry me, Procula. We'll learn about love and marriage together."

That is what happened. We married when the priests determined the time was right – not that Pilate believed in any god, nor did I. But we observed the Roman customs properly. Pilate gave me an emerald necklace, the symbol of rebirth and romance. The soothsayers claimed that emeralds would change color if the wearer was unfaithful. After the affairs of Drusilla, his first wife, maybe Pilate wanted a visible sign of my constant love.

However, as he fastened the clasp, he said, "These emeralds match the sparkle in your eyes."

"My Eros," I murmured, "My god of love."

"My Amor," he answered, and nuzzled my neck.

Our first days were spent at Villa Mirabele while we waited for Pilate's new appointment as Governor of Syria. Others gave us quick glances to see if our marriage bed was – voluptates? Yes, it was. We came to know ourselves – each more passionate and intense than we had guessed. I was amazed (and somewhat amused) by love – that two intelligent people could find themselves in such an odd tangle of arms and legs and hearts, beating together.

My Eros relaxed and gloried that – after so many years alone – he had a wife who cared about him. And I did. I sensed his loneliness that comes with leadership. His decisions seldom pleased everyone. I was fascinated by his experiences and travels. He moved with a confidence that I'd never had – looking so distinguished with his erect bearing and commanding stride. I drew strength from his strength.

For me – I felt the love and passion that I had longed for all my life. I slept with my arm thrown over his shoulder. If I roused at midnight, I felt the warmth of his body against mine, serenely confident of his protection. Were my childhood nightmares gone forever? Maybe. His few snores reminded me of Octavianus. Life is very funny indeed.

Amantes sunt amentes –Lovers are lunatics.

Chapter XVI

P ilate – my Eros – waited through Saturnalia, Januari-us, Februarius and into Martias to hear about his assignment in Syria. He grew morose, even testy.

"Maybe, I'll be passed over," he worried.

"You said that Sejanus promised you an appointment. Government moves slowly. Emperor Tiberius never wanted to lead the Empire. He takes his time on everything. I hear he's bored. He's moving to the Isle of Capri." Pilate didn't respond, so I added, "Just be glad you don't deal with the Senate. There are six-hundreds of them to pass on appointments. At least, you'll need only one approval . . . the Emperor."

Sometimes, Pilate would mutter to himself about his qualifications. "How can I not be named? My citizen status goes back four generations . . . two more than is necessary. My father was of the patrician class. Certainly, the family property at Samnium is sizable enough."

"You have so much vital experience," I added. How dashing my Eros must have looked in his early years as a cavalry commander and cohort leader – a flashing helmet and a polished javelin. Surely, he was a command-ing figure astride a fine spirited steed. When the summons from Sejanus finally came, it was for Martias fifteenth. Pilate became so excited that he didn't realize it was Idus – the historical day when Julius Caesar was assassinated. Like Caesar's wife, Calpurnia, I felt uneasy – unable to concentrate, waiting for his return. Tuum brought me a hot herb drink with honey to soothe my nerves. She spent a long time brushing my hair.

Instead of my dear Eros, an angry Pilate stormed into the room. Something was wrong.

"Well, you are looking at the new Prefect of Judaea, including Samaritis and Idumea!" He gave a cynical laugh and flopped into a chair, like a beaten dog. "Of all the places we could be sent, I'm posted to that quarrelsome region!"

My mind raced to calm him. "Judaea is a neighbor . . . almost . . . to Syria. It may well be preparation for your next post."

Pilate snapped back. "Don't you realize? No one wants Judaea! In fact, Sejanus hates the Jews. Maybe . . . he wants to be rid of me, too. He's assigned me to the most difficult post Roma has. He hopes I'll fail." His jaw tightened as he stared at the floor.

"It must have some stability. Valerius Gratius has governed there for eleven years . . . from the beginning of Tiberius' reign."

"He should have stayed!" Pilate frowned, "Oh, he's had trouble, too! He appointed and dismissed four high priests in as many years. Now, there's one called Caiaphas. It's all infighting or religious quarrels or hatred of the Romans. The place is impossible."

"Well . . . will you turn it down?"

"How can I? There'll be no other post for me if I do."

"It can't be so terrible if the Empire remains at peace."

Pilate interrupted. "That is one thing the Emperor stressed . . ."

"You also had an audience with Tiberius?" I was impressed. Others would be, too.

"Yes! Judaea is one of his personal provinces, a second-class province. Border areas are always restless, and under the Emperor's direction. I report directly to him."

"At least you won't have to answer to the Senate."

"The real military power in the region belongs to Legate Varus of Syria. He has four legions at his command. I have only three thousand mercenaries to help me . . . local soldiers from Caesarea and Samaritis. It'll take some skill to keep them from fighting among themselves. Judaea's coastal cities are filled with Greeks and Syrians, speaking Greek or the Aramaic language and dialects. Interior towns are populated with Yahveh's believers. Both the Judaeans and Samaritans hate each other and the Idumeans are a poor third." Pilate added, moodily. "The whole province seethes with unrest."

"What else did the Emperor say?"

Pilate pointed to each finger, "First. . . I'm to keep peace through persuasion. How easy is that? Second . . . cooperate with the local leaders. Third . . . keep trade moving. *King Herod the Great built Caesarea for a seaport. It is well fortified against piracy, because fourth . . . Tiberius needs the wheat that Judaea exports or there will be bread riots here in Roma." He added, "And fifth . . . of course, taxes. Collect and report revenues."

"Maybe the Judaeans will cooperate if there are no new taxes. Tiberius promised no new taxes."

"It's not that simple. Herod the Great was a builder. You will see not one, but many magnificent marble palaces with lush gardens. He began the great Temple forty years ago. Many artisans still work there. He created Caesarea, the capitol, as a little Roma of white marble." He sighed, "It's all funded with taxes. As Prefect I must collect the money for Herod's projects. That hated tyrant king is dead. Now I'll be the hated tax-collector . . . and ruler!"

"Aren't local citizens are hired as tax-collectors? At least, you won't have to deal with the Judaean complaints directly." I added softly, ". . . Just keep the peace."

"That may be difficult with all the rivalries. The Galileans . . . some are Gentiles . . . sneak in to make trouble, especially those from the Canaanite area. Real fanatics! They live in the north, but they travel to Jerusalem for Passover. We must be there, too, at that time." He paused, "I'm wary of Galilee's Tetrarch, Herod Antipas. He took his father's name. He would love to be called King, too. It's possible that he dreams of a united territory under his rule." Thoughtfully, he stroked his chin. "The Judaeans want to be free. They worship some ancient god called Yahveh, so they despise any ruler like Tiberius. They fiercely object to any census that lists them as Roman subjects."

"What would happen if they gained freedom from Roma?"

"Roma would pay more for much-needed grain which the Judaeans supply." Pilate raised a pointed finger "Listen . . . they fight among themselves . . . Samaritans against rival Judaeans . . . Judaeans against Idumeans! No, it's better if Roma rules and keeps the peace."

I felt a certain sympathy for the Jews. Pilate's remark was similar to the argument by Zio Ammonius – that I had a better life, if he made decisions for me.

Both Pilate and I studied the maps and history of Judaea. When Herod's clan gained power, it allied itself with Roma. The Roman Senate granted a title of King to Herod the Great. Along with his great fortresses and cities, Herod left a legacy of death. He feared plots to depose him – killing his beautiful second wife, Miriamne, their two sons, and most of her family. He also killed Antipater, his heir by his first wife, Doris.

PROCULA | Marion H. Youngquist

When a court eunuch predicted the birth of another new ruler, old Herod killed all Judaean boys under two years old. Some Pharisees balked at a loyalty oath to Emperor Augustus, so King Herod crucified them, too – the worst death for faithful Jews. Protests and riots erupted. Fortunately, old Herod – crazed and ill – died.

Herod's will divide his territory between three favored sons. *Philip II ruled in northeastern Batanaea. Antipas gained both Galilee (north of Samaritis) and Peraea (east of Judaea). Both sons were named as Tetrarchs by Emperor Augustus, meaning each ruled one-fourth of the land.

A third son, *Archaelaus, became Ethnarch over the other half of the region. This included Samaritis, Idumea and Judaea. After official mourning in Roma, Archaelaus returned to Jerusalem. Riots continued there over some martyred Pharisees. As civil strife spread, three thousand people were killed. Governor Varus of Syria marched twenty thousand soldiers into Judaea to restore order. The Temple was burned. The treasury was looted. Two thousand Judaeans were crucified, and thirty-thousand more were sold into slavery. An uneasy peace followed.

For a decade Archaelaus ruled as harshly as his father. Another census sparked a revolt, led by two Galileans, *Judas and Zadok. They encouraged more bloodshed, certain their cause was a righteous one. Anarchy followed. Outlaws roamed everywhere.

Earlier, fifty leaders from Judaea and Samaritis had gone to Roma to meet with Emperor Augustus in the Temple of Apollo. They petitioned him to live according to Yahveh's laws, under a Roman prefect. Finally, Augustus banished Archaelaus to Vienna in Gaul and placed the province under his personal direction. That was two decades ago. Pilate, appointed by Emperor Tiberius, would become the fifth prefect sent out to that difficult place.

Pilate reminded me, "I will represent the Emperor, not only as a tax collector, but as a ruler, general and judge in the eleven districts. I must settle disputes and issue sentences. There will be difficult decisions." He brightened, "Fortunately, the Judaeans and the Sanhedrin will settle their own religious quarrels. I'm no spiritual mediator!"

"It might be wise to know their laws, too."

"You can help. If it pleases you, study their laws and tell me about them."

"How can I read Hebrew?" I asked, amused. As an educated Roman, I knew some classical Greek and spoke *koine* – common Greek. Hebrew would be a challenge.

"Get a tutor. I'm sure some rabbi's son would like to earn a coin or two." He seemed to soften a bit. "You won't mind moving to Caesarea?"

I never belonged in Roma. I was homeless. "Where you go, I go," I said. "Besides, you'll be brilliant. Even the most pious Judaean will love you.

PROCULA | Marion H. Youngquist

You'll go down in history as the perfect Prefect." I kissed his onyx ring, carved with the image of Mars, the god of war. As a soldier, Pilate thought it gave him courage.

"You do believe in me!" Pilate gave a wry smile. "I'll be lucky if I'm remembered even for a decade."

"Perhaps –," I chided him, "– Or perhaps longer." I remembered a line from history –Post cineres gloria sera. Glory comes after one is reduced to ashes.

Pilate reflected a moment. "The important thing is to rule firmly, justly, and wisely. I have the power of the Emperor behind me. The Judaeans have no army . . . no weapons. Nothing. They depend on religion and it has no power. They will soon realize that mighty Roma is invincible!"

I didn't argue, but – like many men – Pilate didn't know everything. The Judaeans placed their confidence in Yahveh. Was their belief more powerful than the Roman sword? Was there an answer in that far-off land?

I needed to do two things before I left Roma. In her illness, I discovered how much Tuum loved Roma. Now she was a young woman with delicate features – thin nose, high cheekbones and still those luminous dark eyes. Intelligent, she quickly assessed new situations. She had been my playmate, my companion, my helper and my confidant. As difficult as it would be, I knew she deserved her freedom. Immediately, Lucius would hire her to run the households when I left.

We sat in the garden and recalled the fables, the flute lessons, our pantomimes – all the funny and sad experiences that we shared for over a decade.

"Tuum, if you wish to stay in Roma, you can." I turned away, so she wouldn't see my tears. "I grant you your freedom."

Silence.

"Bibi! Don't you want me anymore?"

"Of course, I do. Soon, we will sail to a strange land. I don't know when we will return. You love Roma . . ."

"A long time ago, I begged you not to send me away. I repeat, forever . . . YOU are my Bibi. I will go faraway with YOU."

I reminded her, "You are free."

"Not now. Someday. I am still your slave. You can't do your hair without me. You need me when the bad dreams come."

We sat with clasped hands for a long time in silence.

Before we left Roma, Zio Ammonius called me to his library. In his stilted manner, he thanked me again for Zia Terentia's care. "I know our relationship has been strained, but I hope we can part, feeling kindlier toward each other."

I ignored his remark. Boldly, I said, "I want my dowry returned to me."

"Are you sure? I've tried to manage it wisely."

"I want to manage my money myself!"

Even Lucius raised his eyebrows at my request. In a few days, Zio Ammonius bought Villa Mirabele, and converted my investments into cash. I opened an account in the banking firm of Balbus and Ollius. I made Lucius my agent.

I felt a certain power from my large sum of money – larger than I expected. Zio Ammonius had been a good steward on my behalf. However, I wasn't grateful. When he opened his arms to give me a farewell hug, I walked past him without even a peasant Gratia. He winced. I left him standing there.

I never saw him again.

Chapter XVII

We sailed by ship in late Maius of 779 a.u.c.1 – ab urbe condita – years counted from the first year when Roma was founded. It was the twelfth year of Tiberius' reign. Winds and the gods determined our sailing date. I worried because of a nightmare – that the ship lost its anchor. Tuum calmed me because her dream – of walking on water – was a good sign. Together, the omens canceled each other. Also, Pilate gave me a garnet ring which would protect me from nightmares and from danger while traveling.

Pilate bought himself an aquamarine amulet as a protection against sea monsters as well as marital discord. However, there was no problem between us – only excitement about the future. Pilate brought along Clodius as his personal aide – not a slave like Tuum – but an assistant like Lucius. Clodius supervised our space on the bireme, a naval ship. Nearby ships held seven-gallonamphora, filled with wine and olive oil, important exports. The clay pots came from Arretium, a good omen to me. Olive oil was used in cooking as well as cosmetics, ointments for wounds, lamp lights, bathing, and religious rituals.

The winds determined our route. We crossed the great sea, south to Alexandria. Cargo was unloaded. Linen, pepper, paper and glass were brought aboard. We continued east and northward to Caesarea, the capitol of Judaea.

PROCULA | Marion H. Youngquist

Caesarea had a long and honorable history, developed as a seaport by the Phoenicians. Caesarea was given to King Herod the Great by Emperor Augustus. Near the end of his life, Herod constructed a new white marble city within twelve years. Its people included a mixture of Jews, Greeks, Syrians, and AEgyptians. If buildings were in Roman style, Greek influence dominated the city's culture.

When we docked I was thrilled. A fifty-acre basin held a breakwater, some twenty-five hundred feet in circumference. The long pier jutted two-hundred feet into the sea. Several watchtowers added to the impressive entrance with its round turret and twin columns. The city was a pivotal port for trade.

From Parthia in the east and Petraea, south, camel caravans brought silk from the orient, cotton and spices from the Indies and perfumes from Nabataea. Judaea exported barley, wheat, plums, figs and balsam, along with bitumen from the Dead Sea. The province's well-laden ships were necessary if Roma's inhabitants were to be fed.

On a far hill, the Temple of Augustus glistened in the brilliant sun. From a map, I knew there was a theater in the south end of town and an amphitheater in the northeast. Obviously, King Herod had copied Roma. With half its population being Greek, Caesarea was a Hellenized city in every way.

Pilate's headquarters were in Herod's luxurious palace. The citadel would protect us from any revolt. Spacious marble halls were paved with mosaics. But where were the costly furnishings – inlaid tables, golden goblets, and marble statuary? Were rumors true? Was King Herod a robber of ancient royal tombs? Where were the artifacts? Evidently, Pilate's predecessor, Valerius Gratus, shipped many of those precious objects back to Roma with his own personal effects. I saw immediately that I had a huge task to do. For the first time in my life, I could decorate rooms as I pleased.

The gardens were shabby, but remnants of exotic flower beds and ornate fountains were visible. A few white doves and brilliant peacocks lingered there. If I could find some capable workers, life would be very good in Judaea. Maybe Herod's palace was the castle-by-the-sea that Guiseppi had predicted for me so long ago.

When Tuum and I explored the city, we realized it was very cosmopolitan. Syrian merchants, Greek shipowners, even Roman bankers and Oriental artisans resided there. Many Judaeans, also, had small shops. I found a fine sandal maker on a side street. He fitted Tuum and me with soft slippers.

Often Tuum and I shopped at the wharf, buying silk scarves from the orient and fine perfumes from Petraea. We lingered among spices from the

Indies. The finest linen came from AEgyptus. Pilate and Clodius strolled along the waterfront, tossing coins to young divers.

Within a few months, Pilate ordered a stone from the Kabbara quarry, north of the capitol. The huge monument, almost square, was inscribed:

> *Pontius Pilate, Prefect of Judaea, has given*
> *this Tiberieum to the citizens of Caesarea.*

In this way, the names of Pilate and Tiberius were together in a clever political move. It was installed in the new civic hall. Would Tiberius, who resisted honors, hear about it on Capri – his pleasure isle?

We arrived in Caesarea after Passover that spring. Fortunately, it had been observed in Jerusalem with peace and dignity. The Galilean pilgrims didn't make trouble. Only a few Roman troops were on site – only those stationed there at Fort Antonio. Pilate was relieved that there was no immediate crisis.

With Tuum's help, I set about creating a warm atmosphere in the Caesarea palace. Rather than order furniture and art from Roma, I decided to use local artisans.

Pilate advised, "A centurion, Cornelius, is stationed here. He's married to Esther, a Jewess who was raised in Caesarea. She'll know the local trades people."

Esther came the next afternoon. She was a short trim woman, only a little older than I. Her thick dark hair was pulled back from her smooth cheeks by silver combs. Her manner was cordial but reserved. She studied Tuum and me with perceptive brown eyes. She would not deceive me, but I dare not misuse her trust.

I wanted rugs for the cold marble floors. Esther led us down alleyways to the Syrian rug sellers whom she knew. Pilate sent along Clodius to haggle over prices. This amused me, as I remembered Lucius' techniques with merchants. Lucius looked for flaws – real or imagined. Size – too small or too large. Color, texture – anything to delay the sale, until the tradesman reduced his price. I would do the same and let Clodius watch me.

Tuum whispered, "Bibi . . . while you talk to a merchant, let me help. I'll turn over a corner of the rug. I learned from my mean old master how yarns should be knotted or if the fringe is correctly tied. I can tell if the yarn is properly dyed."

So the four of us – Clodius, Esther, Tuum and myself – spent several mornings with rug merchants. Esther sometimes acted as interpreter, but I negotiated the price. When I placed an order, word quickly spread. Esther chose honest merchants to show us their wares. Soon, rugs and some small marble tables appeared in the large drafty rooms. Benches with wrought iron legs lined the long entrance hall. Couches and carved chairs with curved backs were placed for conversational groups in the reception room. Damask pillows were added everywhere, so that people could relax in comfort.

Tuum laughed, "Bibi, let's open a business. I know quality. I'll buy. You sell."

"Our own business?" I grinned. "Sure! With a BIG sign . . . House of Tuum and Bibi."

"No . . . Bibi and Tuum!" she said, reaching out to shake my hand in an imaginary partnership.

I wanted, particularly, a large wall painting for the entrance hall, done in the Roman style. Esther brought me Apollonius, son of the Greek sculptor in Roma. He'd drifted to Caesarea to establish his reputation as a painter, apart from his famous father. We discussed a subject.

"I would like a scene of a famous tale from the region's history . . . a pastoral scene." I added, "I want the palace to reflect the heritage of the area."

A look passed between Esther and the artist. He promised sketches within a week, as it was a big commission and he was anxious to be paid. He came back with a drawing of a shepherd boy, holding a lamb. A slingshot was at his waist. He stood by a tree, beside a stream. In the far distance some men approached. I assumed they were the boy's friends or brothers.

"How charming," I said. "It will do very well. Be sure to use soft shades of green on the trees. I don't want anything too stark." I turned away. Should a patron tell the artist how to paint? My remark embarrassed me.

Apollonius finished his painting within six weeks. Tuum thought it was stunning. Even Pilate pronounced it a good job in his best military voice. Soon, I found out that it depicted David, a young shepherd, who killed Goliath, a foreign invader. Was there a hidden message on the wall for the Roman army? I didn't ask. I paid his fee. Pilate was ignorant of the story and said nothing.

With a calm spirit –aequo animo– I said nothing either.

Two weeks later, we were in our bedroom. Pilate slept at night without any clothing. He enjoyed being free from his uniform. I massaged his back with oil of myrrh.

"Procula," he propped his head in his hand, "I hesitate to tell you this. I found out that the hall painting is of a Jewish hero, King David, as a boy. He defeated a huge enemy warrior, Goliath. It's an insult to us . . . the enemy, the Roman occupation army."

I feigned surprise. "Really? I thought you liked it."

"I do!" said Pilate. "Leave it. It may give us some extra credibility . . . that we're appreciative of Judaean history. I thought you should know, "he said, kissing my hand. "You're such an innocent."

I smiled and kissed the top of his head.

Chapter XVIII

By mid-summer, Pilate began his agenda. He toured the districts twice a year to review court cases and assess any needs. We went to Jerusalem at sacred times – Passover, the Feast of Unleavened Bread, and Shavuot – the Festival of the Weeks, and Succoth– the Feast of the Tabernacles. He maintained peace and order while the Judaeans observed their rites. It was a simple and reasonable approach – a workable plan. Also, Pilate wanted people to realize that he would rule justly and fairly as the new Prefect. However, he miscalculated the Judaeans religious fervor and his own strength and wisdom.

Elsewhere in the Empire, Tiberius' image graced buildings and monuments. Coins were stamped with his profile. At celebrations, the army marched with gold medallions, a half-foot in diameter, attached to their standards. It was Tiberius' face, wreathed by a border, that gleamed in the sun and sent golden rays over an awed crowd. Many Romans worshiped dead rulers, like Augustus, and built temples in their honor. Tiberius was still alive and must be honored – so Pilate believed.

In Judaea things were different. The Judaeans worshiped Yahveh. They had a strong prohibition against sacred images. The Emperor's face was abhorred because he might claim to be a god, just as Caesar Augustus was called a messiah.

Pilate acted quickly to honor Tiberius and show the Judaeans that he was a strong ruler. He sent troops into Jerusalem after midnight, where they placed the medallions of Tiberius on Fort Antonio's walls, next to the sacred Temple. There, the Judaeans saw them, gleaming gold – rich and decorative – in the morning sun. Although no previous prefect had attempted this, Pilate was sure the Judaeans would be impressed by their beauty. It also seemed clever as the weather had turned cooler and there were fewer pilgrims – especially Galileans – in Jerusalem who might object. Pilate was wrong.

A week later, we awoke to a noisy crowd outside the palace. Pilate sent word that he would not meet with anyone until after breakfast and his bath. He took his time. Why should the prefect of a visible state be hurried by the followers of an invisible god?

Tuum and I crept to a window. Down below, we saw men from Jerusalem who had trudged some fifteen furlongs to protest any medallions in their holy city. Some had their feet bound in rags, cloaks held tightly against their thin bodies shivering in the cold air. The Sandal maker and the Coppersmith of Caesarea were also there with other local Judaeans. Although they were influenced by Greek culture, they remained loyal to their faith and their Jerusalem brothers.

Caiaphas, the Jerusalem high priest who gained his position through bribery, was not in the crowd. No doubt he and the *Sanhedrin had organized the protest. Over the next five days, Tuum and I often stood in an anteroom and listened to Pilate negotiate with the Judaeans, who begged to be understood. They prayed for his heart to change.

"Your Excellency . . . we beg you . . . take down the standards. According to our laws, they are an abomination to Elohim and to us," said a tall Judaean spokesman.

"You can keep your laws in your temple and in your homes. The Emperor's laws keeps the peace. The standards belong to the army. They're displayed on a Roman fort. They're beautiful. They will remain." Pilate dismissed them.

Daily, the Judaeans asked Pilate to reconsider. He became testier. His jaw tightened, and he snapped at the palace steward, a Judaean, when his stew was too salty. Even Clodius didn't bring his reports fast enough.

On the sixth day, Pilate was at the Circus races. He entered with his aides and a great fanfare of trumpets to emphasize Roman presence. He tossed out his personal coins, minted with alituus – an augur's wand, used to predict the future. On the other side, the coins bore a wreath with berries, centered with three barley ears. Although the coins lacked images, the Judaeans didn't like them. Pilate's mint wasn't allowed within the Temple court in Jerusalem where the money-changers sat.

The upset Judaeans followed Pilate to the stadium. They shook their fists and refused to leave until he settled their case. He was the magistrate who must decide.

"Roma rules!" Pilate said. "Remember, the Emperor banished your people from Roma five years ago! I can do the same to you! Go away!"

"Elohim rules forever!" they cried.

Then, Pilate threatened them with gladii – punishment with a sword. He could wound and kill because he was also a military commander.

"Elohim rules forever!" they repeated in unison.

"As the Emperor's Prefect, I have the power of life and death! Crucifixion is for those who defy and plot against the Emperor! You will be nailed to a cross! Go away!"

It was a powerful threat, because the Judeans believed that crucifixion meant that Yahveh had abandoned them. They whispered among themselves. The next day was their Shabbat, when they would again meet Yahveh in prayer. They would not break Yahveh's law against images. They stood together.

Silence.

An old bearded rabbi came forward, his body shaking. "Your Excellency," he said, firmly and quietly, "We are ready to die. Either take down the standards or kill us all."

Pilate stared at him in disbelief. The Judaeans had to be mad to give their lives for some unseen god. He had grown tired of them all. It would never do for Sejanus – or Tiberius on Capri – to hear of a mass execution within his first year as prefect. Two decades ago, Archaelaus had lost his rule because of a massacre.

I knew how Pilate would react. He would think, *I must save any show of force for greater firebrands than these devout peasants, especially since Tiberius has advised his representatives to be "good shepherds".*

"Clodius, order the standards to be returned to Caesarea." Pilate turned to the Judaeans, "Get out!" An enraged Pilate ignored everyone and went to bed early.

Clodius described the confrontation to Tuum and me. For Pilate, it remained a closed subject. He found, very quickly, that being the Prefect of Emperor Tiberius would not be an easy task. That was our introduction to a powerful example of faith by devoted followers of Yahveh. Judaea had a population of two and a half-million people. A hundred thousand lived in Jerusalem. Most were as faithful to Yahveh as the protesters.

Herod the Great had erected magnificent edifices, copied from Roma. Yet, the Judaeans refused to adopt any enlightened Roman ways. If Romans wore togas or tunics and were clean-shaven, the Judaeans dressed in rough-spun robes and wore beards. They showed open contempt for

Roman culture. The Judaeans scorned Roman history, which covered only eight centuries from the founding of Roma. Their ancient history covered twenty-five centuries, back to Abraham and – through Yahveh – to the beginning of time. They belonged only to Yahveh, a supreme deity completely different and superior to all Roman gods. Once, they had been enslaved in AEgyptus. Never again would they bow to any earthly ruler – or be Roman citizens. They intended to be free.

If Pilate was furious with the Judaeans, I was curious about such devotion to Yahveh. They waited for the first evening star to begin Shabbat, finding warmth and closeness in their songs and rituals. They had an inner joy about heaven and earth that captivated me. No god claimed me, but they belonged to Yahveh.

Three weeks later, I knew my announcement would help Pilate forget about the golden standards. I was with child as the Judaeans phrased it. Tuum clapped her hands and immediately fussed over me.

"Here's a pillow. Put your feet up and rest. We'll go to the garden and watch the peacocks. Close your eyes and dream a little," Tuum said. She had a dozen instructions.

Esther came, beaming as well. "A mother is twice blessed . . . for a child is a gift from Yahveh and she will always be loved by her children."

Pilate simply said, "A son! At last, a son. A man is immortal through a son!"

"What if we have a daughter?" I asked, half-afraid.

That stopped him. He slowly answered, "She will be as beautiful as her mother . . . my own precious jewel. Everyone will envy me!"

That night, Pilate brought me a sparkling ruby bracelet for long life and health. I felt supremely happy. Tuum said my face glowed like a morning sunrise.

I decided the best way for Pilate to recover from the awkward confrontation was to give a banquet. Caesarea's leaders could see the beauty of their refurbished palace. It would lift Pilate's spirits. Others would see him as affable and charming. His past public dispute would be remembered as a quarrel with conservative religious protestors from Jerusalem – not with the tolerant cultured people of Caesarea.

Invitations were sent to a variety of people – ship owners, the quarry owner, several rabbis, a perfume seller, competing rug merchants, a linen importer, landowners, poets, philosophers and artists. The wives were included, too. This was a surprise to many people. All our slaves were dressed alike in new apparel which excited them. They provided extra care in washing the hands and feet of new arrivals at our party. A laurel wreath was placed on each guest's head (except the rabbis). Lavender perfume was sprinkled on their hair.

Tuum suggested that a lyre be played near the entrance hall, so lovely tunes would be heard as the guests entered. We had a flute player during the banquet. Also, a local poet read an "Ode to the Prefect". It went on a bit long, but then poets are never short of words. Satis verborum – enough of words. A magician performed tricks.

I was anxious for the gardens to be more presentable. The head gardener had left to return to his home in Hebron. Fortunately, an old gardener – who had served during the last years of King Herod's reign--had a grandson he could instruct. He sat like Herod, himself, near the central pool and gave the young man advice and instruction. Bushes were neatly trimmed. The fountains were cleaned out. Soon, sunlit sprays emerged to delight future guests with the gentle sight and sound of water music.

Esther and Apollonius brought a stonemason to see me. He supplied some small carved animals for accent pieces. Although there were few flowers, the gardens flourished when the day arrived. Tuum suggested oil lamps be placed along the paths, so everything had a festive air as the evening stars appeared.

When Pilate frowned about my requisition list, I revised it. I purchased some things from my dowry funds – such as the round inlaid table for the reception hall. It was jewel-like with stones laid and polished to represent a wreath of flowers. I also bought large brass urns which Tuum suggested. They held small palms and stood beside the marble columns in the grand hall. I was sure that I would carry these treasures along to any future home.

Tuum and I considered different dishes for the menu. We eliminated pork, so we wouldn't offend any Judaean guest. We made sure that no food was prepared in pans that been previously used for swine. The lamb was roasted to succulent perfection and served with mint jelly.

We served small bread rounds spread with goat cheese from Sicily. Fortunately, a ship from Hispania arrived, so we had secured artichokes and pickled fish. We ordered truffles from Jerusalem. They gave a delicate flavor to the deviled eggs. These were centered with huge bowls of olives. Proudly, I pointed out that the red-glazed bowls were from Arretium. There were trays of grapes, plums and figs from local growers. The kitchen staff had stuffed dates with nutmeats. Apollonius suggested a Greek pastry confection filled with nutmeats and honey.

PROCULA | Marion H. Youngquist

There were many toasts with Pilate's imported red wine from Gaul. We made sure that local wines were also served. One set of glass goblets came from Syria and the other, AEgyptus. People dressed in their finest clothing. Over a basic white linen tunic with a belt or sash, they wore a mantle, sometimes caught on the shoulder with a gold or jeweled brooch. Pilate decided to wear a robe with a purple band, instead of a Roman toga, in respect for local custom. We knew a man was Judaean if he wore a fringe at the hem of his robe.

That night, I chose a yellow silk mantle, jeweled along the edges. Tuum spent a long time on my hair. She fashioned curls on top and secured them with pins of gold and ivory. I added an emerald-studded headband and my emerald necklace. I glittered, in a way unusual for me, but as the hostess and Prefect's wife it was expected that I should easily be recognized. My growing abdomen was barely noticeable.

I met guests at the door. I made sure all were included in some conversation. I walked with them through the gardens. I saw their silver plates were never empty. In every way it appeared to be a successful evening. I remembered Zia Terentia and made sure that my hospitality was genuine and gracious.

Pilate whispered that the party marked a new acceptance and cordial relations between local citizens and Roman occupation. Many guests had never been in the palace. Around the rooms, compliments were offered. I recalled the saying *pessimum genus inimicorum laudantes* – flatterers are the worst kind of enemies.

Just as the last guests were leaving, I felt a dampness, an oozing, slide down my legs. I said a hasty Good-night and turned away from Pilate's scowl and the guests surprised looks. Tuum followed me quickly upstairs. I fell across my bed, afraid of what I knew for certain. I was hemorrhaging. I started to cry. People came and left at Tuum's direction. Esther rushed in with a Judaean midwife. My legs were raised. I was given a potion and slept. My last memory is of Pilate in the doorway with a stunned look before he turned away.

Weeks of confinement followed. If the baby moved, I was fearful of a premature birth. If it didn't move, I was afraid it was dead. When I became depressed, Tuum played her flute and read to me. Pilate would talk a little about his day and then leave my room. He had a hard time expressing his concern. He always wanted to appear strong and commanding. This he couldn't control.

I knew Pilate didn't like to change his plans. Even though things were different for me, he still meant to go to Jerusalem for the Passover season with his troops. I would not be with him. I didn't want him to go.

"Stay with me," I pleaded, half-fearing what I knew could happen.

"I can't, Procula." Pilate turned away. "The Emperor said firmly that I must be in Jerusalem for each Passover. There's always a possibility of riots. I can't issue an order from Caesarea to prevent trouble that far away."

"It's always what the Emperor commands!" I angrily muttered, under my breath.

After the strained conversation, he gave me a brief kiss and left. I turned my face to the wall and wept. I lost my faith that he would ever give me support in time of need. I knew my body was losing the contest of time.

The next night, my water broke. The midwife rushed in to assist at the birth. Our tiny daughter, premature, was born at dawn. I named her Aurora. The midwife cut the navel cord, bathed Aurora, rubbed her with salt and wrapped her in swaddling bands. She placed her gently in my arms. I rocked and crooned to her, tears running down my cheeks. Tuum, the midwife, two slaves, and the others cried with me. After a time, the midwife took her away. She and Tuum wrapped Aurora in a soft blanket and placed her in a rock cave where other infants were buried. Aurora's eyes were closed forever against a warring world, cruelty and pain.

I spent several weeks recovering. The slaves were kind but said nothing. I bore my sorrow with Stoic calm, but in my heart, I grieved. I put my ruby bracelet away. Was Pilate sad? I didn't know. He had a hard time expressing his feelings. Did he think Aurora's death was my fault? Some inherited weakness? A small rift came between us. I resented his imperial manner, his cynical view of life and of other people.

There was a new steeliness in Pilate's eyes if Clodius and the servants didn't respond fast enough to his commands. Did he spend a longer time away on judicial trips? Without a son, who would remember him in the annual ancestor rites? Or build a temple in his memory? These questions troubled me, but we did not discuss them.

Ovid wrote, *temporis ars medicina fere est* —time is a great healer. I waited.

I wrote to Lucius about Aurora's birth and death. Two weeks later, a courier brought his reply.

To Procula, esteemed wife of Pontius Pilate –

It grieves me to hear of Aurora's death, for there is great sadness with any death, especially the loss of a dear child. I wish I were there to comfort you.

PROCULA | Marion H. Youngquist

There are changes in Roma. Julius and Iris are divorced. She and the children continue to live on the Capitoline. Your uncle determined that Julius was not suited for banking. He sent Julius to Villa Fortunata. He hopes the country air can help him.

My life has changed, too. Soon, I will leave Roma. Your uncle no longer needs me. Recently I was in Alexandria to complete some business for him. I decided to buy a house there. Things are unsettled in Roma, so I also invested in rental property for you. You must visit your new real estate sometime. We will go to the famous Library. I know that you love libraries.

Your friend, Lucius

From Iris, I received a curt and bitter note.

Procula – My marriage is over. Julius drank too much and had too many affairs. So now I have to raise three children by MYSELF. You won't have that struggle. You'll still be popular. Like Seneca says," with us, childlessness gives more power than it takes away." Enjoy yourself. I wish I could.
Iris

I kept Lucius' letter.

Chapter XIX

The next spring, we traveled to Jerusalem at Passover time. The city was calm, and the joyful observance passed without difficulty. We continued southward through Judaea, stopping at fortress palaces like Herodium, high on a conical hill. From there we visited Masada, near the Dead Sea's western shore. It was a true fortified castle on a boat-shaped mountain some thirteen hundred feet above the arid desert. The trip was difficult, snaking up the mountain, especially for the litter bearers. Poor Tuum and Clodius were on pack animals. Tuum was exhausted for two days.

Herod the Great constructed Masada for his personal use. A lovely villa stood apart from the main palace and community facilities. One terrace jutted out on the northern cliff while two others, reached by a narrow rock-hewn passageway, were below. The vista was breathtaking. I think that Pilate, too, felt invincible, ruling from such an isolated and majestic peak. Nothing could touch us there. From the heights, we saw a string of army posts, stretching for several miles. We stayed for three days. The return downhill was easier, descending in the early morning when it was cooler.

We continued northward toward Jericho, arriving at a stadia near the Jordan River. A crowd stood nearby, beneath blooming locust trees filled with swarming bees. Pilate was always suspicious of groups and curious about their leaders. He knew Judaean history was filled with attempts by outlaw bands to raid the Temple or steal from royal graves. Often, a hothead claimed to be a new king or messiah. Pilate wryly said that his greatest challenge was to save the Judaeans from more fiery leaders who felt called by Yahveh to rescue his people.

When our entourage stopped, he sent Clodius to investigate. I was glad to leave the carriage and stretch. Even with goose-down pillows, the ride was uncomfortable. Tuum scrambled down first to assist me. I called to Clodius to wait. The three of us walked toward the river. Pilate went into the inn for refreshment with the cavalry captain.

Cautiously, a few people moved aside as we drew near. Although nothing was said, I saw their stony silent stares. A man, wearing a rough camel's hair tunic and a leather girdle, stood farther out in the water. Later, we heard he was John the Baptist, living in the manner of an ascetic who ate wild honey and dried locust pods.

"I am not Elijah!" he thundered. "I am the voice of one crying in the wilderness. Repent! Repent! You brood of vipers! You are as sinful as Herod Antipas. He has stolen his brother's wife. And she is a Jewish mother with a Jewish child! Remember . . . every tree that does not bear good fruit will be cut down and thrown into the fire!" He called out, "I baptize you with water, but the Messiah is coming! He will baptize you with the Holy Spirit and with fire. Beg for the forgiveness of your sins. Repent! Repent!"

The crowd began to question the preacher. He answered that they must share their food and clothing with the poor, and tax-collectors must be honest.

Clodius, mesmerized by the speaker's fervent delivery, cried out, ". . . And what are we soldiers to do?" Embarrassed by his emotional response, Clodius rubbed his shoe in the sand.

The preacher replied, "Rob no one by violence or by false accusation! And be content with your wages!"

It was obvious he was some kind of seer or prophet. A few people waded into the water and immersed themselves. The rough-clad man poured water over their heads three times and prayed. Was baptism a local variation of purification rites? The cleansed ones came out tearful and smiling, murmuring about being forgiven. What sins? These were simple peasants struggling to survive on small plots, owned by wealthy landowners.

We saw the intensity in the eyes of John the Baptist as he attacked Antipas. I thought it was good that he was preaching in Judaea, under Pilate's protection. In Galilee or Peraea, he would be arrested for attacking the Tetrarch. We had yet to meet that Fox as others called him.

PROCULA | Marion H. Youngquist

That afternoon was farthest from my mind when, a few months later, Pilate received an official invitation from Herod Antipas to a state banquet at the Machaerus Palace. It was a double celebration – Antipas' birthday and the fifteenth year of Tiberius' reign.

I was excited to see the Black Fortress, as it was called, because of its history. Many centuries old and located in Peraea deep in the mountains east of the Dead Sea, it was rebuilt by Herod the Great. Often Pilate studied the maps and commented how easily Antipas could threaten Judaea's northern and eastern borders. Only the Roman occupation kept that wily Fox from reclaiming Judaea. If the Judaeans ever rallied to him, he'd persuade Roma to crown him King Herod the Great, II.

Pilate couldn't refuse the invitation, but he prepared – carefully. He took extra troops with him, using the excuse that the mountain terrain demanded more personnel. I accompanied him because my presence would make the banquet a social occasion, rather than two provincial rulers verbally sparring with each other.

I heard that Herod's wife was vain – like Zia Terentia. No one dared be more beautiful than Herodias. I remembered my aunt's sparkling rings and wondered if Herodias wore two handfuls. I left my emerald necklace in the case and wore silver bracelets, anklets and a heavy chain necklace. Was my gown too plain? Would Herodias find me amusing or dull?

Pilate called my worries foolish. "Just have Tuum do your hair with a circlet of orange blossoms on top and you'll be the regalest one there. I'll have to keep you away from old Antipas. He may try to grab you, too," he said, and hugged me.

Pilate was delayed when two couriers arrived with documents from Caesarea. He decided I should go on to the banquet. He would follow later and make a grand entrance with a flourish of drums and trumpets, offering his respects to Antipas in a ceremony that honored the Emperor, too.

I sat in the great hall, admiring the golden frieze, carved doors and columns. Tuum stood behind me to check quietly on what I was served. Would Antipas dare poison the prefect's wife? He could offer his young step-daughter, Salome, as my replacement. That would be a political union to cement relations between Galilee and Judaea!

Antipas kept signaling for   glasses to be refilled. Meanwhile, Herodias clapped her hands and ordered entertainment. Smiling, she pushed Salome forward to dance. As an honored guest, I had to appear appreciative – even enthusiastic – at the sad spectacle of a dancer without talent. Antipas grew tipsier and more ordered the musicians, "Shplay!"

Salome jiggled her finger bells, missing the drummer's beat. Awkwardly, she shuffled to mime a story. When her exotic mask slipped, and her scarlet veil fell from her shoulders, Antipas applauded gleefully, so the guests clapped, too.

"Sh-take shwhat sh-you want of my sh-kingdom!" he drunkenly shouted to Salome.

Antipas, Salome and Herodias whispered together as the guests anticipated the meal. The aroma prepared us for roast lamb and oryza. Crystal bowls held tomatoes and olives. Sweet figs and pears nestled on silver plates. I saw an aide of Antipas and some soldiers leave the room. Was it time for Pilate to appear and the ceremony to begin?

I slipped out on the balcony for fresh air and to brace myself for the charade of two rivals meeting each other. When I came back, I found fresh trays of sweets. I had just taken a few grapes, when the chaos started. The musicians lifted their trumpets. I expected a warm and special greeting. Instead, a servant came in with a huge silver platter, on which rested the head of the prophet, John the Baptist – his dead eyes glaring as wildly as they had at the Jordan River.

I screamed and fainted – and many others did, too. Herodias rushed out, followed by Antipas, drunk and unsteady, held up by two guards. Their welcome ceremony for Pilate never took place. Wisely, Pilate decided on an early departure the next day. I took back to Caesarea a recurring nightmare of a bloodied head on a silver platter.

Sleeping through every night was difficult. Tuum gave me various potions. Pilate, weary, firmly advised – with some irritation – that I get over it. So, I hid my restlessness with other excuses – indigestion, too much sun, a difficult servant, or a quarrelsome tradesman. I even took up the flute again for solace. However, I lost heart and found relief from my headaches only when Tuum played.

Pilate grew moody, staring into space. He was still angry over the forced removal of the standards from Jerusalem. Maybe the loss of our daughter also filled his mind. By a chance remark, I provided Pilate with a new project. It occupied him so intensely that the medallion mistake became history.

During the hot summer, I was always thirsty. The merciless sun beat down on us and dried up any moisture on our tongues. Tuum and I would return from the market and drink several goblets of water. She cooled my forehead with a damp towel. Later, when I listened to Hebrew praise-songs,

I fully understood the meaning of the river of Yahveh is full of water. It contained both a promise and blessing for his people in Judaea.

When we arrived in Jerusalem that fall for Succoth or the Feast of Tabernacles, the city was suffering from drought. Cisterns and pools were dangerously low. The palace steward advised us that water was being rationed. That was especially hard for Pilate who enjoyed his daily bath as a time of relaxation. As we discussed the situation that night, I said, "What Jerusalem needs is a good Roman aqueduct, better than the two that King Herod built."

Pilate stared at me for a moment and pounded his fist, "Procula, that's brilliant! That's the answer! An aqueduct! The citizens of Jerusalem will send their gratification all the way to Roma if they have a never-ending supply of fresh clear water."

". . . But the cost? The Judaeans will rebel over any new taxes."

Pilate, thinking, turned his wine glass slowly and tapped his foot. "The Temple treasury overflows with money."

". . . But that's corban. . . holy money."

"It comes from all over the Empire. Remember how Tiberius was angry when the Jews in Roma sent money here to the Jerusalem temple? He will be pleased if I use corban for this project." Pilate drew imaginary aqueduct arches with his spoon. "Think of how many good causes are funded by the Temple. What is a better one than to guarantee water . . . pure clean water . . . for everyone?"

"It won't be easy to convince *Caiaphas, the high priest . . . or the Sanhedrin . . . to grant funds for a Roman aqueduct."

Pilate gave a wry smile. "Caiaphas was handed his position by Roma. Herod the Great began the custom of appointing the high priests. When he died, the Emperor's staff assumed that duty. I will remind Caiaphas that as Roma gives, Roma can take away." He paused, "The Sanhedrin won't object. They'll see how helpful it can be. No doubt someone will start a new business . . . selling water from the Wadi springs! I can hear the hawkers now . . . Fresh water blessed by the high priest!" Pilate wore a cynical smile.

And that is how it happened. Pilate sent for Caiaphas and some prominent leaders – among them, Joseph of Arimathea, who owned vast land holdings, and Nicodemus, one of the three richest men in Jerusalem.

Joseph of Arimathea counseled Pilate to grant some tax relief, however small, as a gesture of good-will and to offset any criticism of using Temple money. So, Pilate rescinded the grain-tax for one year. Joseph was pleased as his harvested crops were directly affected. Indirectly, Nicodemus benefited too, as farmers had more money to spend at his various import stands.

That was the beginning of a two-year project – a wonderful focus for Pilate. He assembled his engineers and troops to complete the original plan begun by Herod the Great. Pilate's aqueduct, lined with lead and lime mortar, ran for some three-hundred furlongs, linking the southern springs in the Wadi el Arab to Solomon's pools near Bethlehem. From there, Herod's two great high-and-low level aqueducts carried water into Jerusalem.

Pilate expected that the Judaeans would honor him, now that fresh water was guaranteed. However, grumbling began when his project cut through an old cemetery. According to custom, that made the water unclean. Some said the aqueduct was a Roman monstrosity, despoiling holy ground. Even tax relief was discounted as too-long in coming. Pilate discovered there was no way to gain the trust of the Judaeans. He held his temper, but inwardly he seethed with rage.

When Pilate went up to Jerusalem for the next festival, he faced an angry crowd. He sat regally in his tribunal – the chair he used as a Roman magistrate. He wore his white toga, banded in purple, to remind them of his position. Two guards stood beside him. That didn't deter the shouting crowd who clenched their fists and hurled epithets – "Roman dog! Pig! Evil One!" When some spit, his clean robe was splattered.

However, Pilate had prepared for the mob. Some soldiers were disguised in native dress with head cloths and false beards. They concealed clubs and daggers thrust in the folds of their robes. When Pilate saw the crowd surge forward, he gave a signal. His hidden soldiers swung right and left, while people screamed and ran. Pilate stood erect and left the bloody melee quickly. He retired to our suite and canceled all meetings for that day.

Pilate was uneasy. If the Emperor heard about the unrest, he might recall his Prefect. So, Pilate waited for any official warning or dismissal. None came. How could the Sanhedrin send a protest to Tiberius when they had first agreed to fund the aqueduct?

Pecunia obediunt olet. All things are obedient to money.

Pilate went on another judicial circuit but expected to return in time for his birthday. I wanted to give him some special slippers, woolly-lined, to wander through our marble halls. Tuum and I went to the Sandal maker, a poor Judaean with several sons and a baby daughter. His shop was near the quay so that sailors and travelers could easily buy his inexpensive footwear.

His place was closed – a surprise since it was a weekday morning and not Shabbat. Tuum inquired from the Basket weaver next door. His stiff manner and curt voice let us know that we were adversaries – unwanted Roman women in a hostile land.

"The Sandal maker has taken his family to Capernaum in Galilee. He heard that a rabbi with healing power was there. He might help his baby daughter. Little Miriam is slowly dying from lack of nourishment. She can't swallow her mother's milk." He added, "My poor friends have tried everything. This is their last hope."

I admired the Sandal maker for his genuine concern. I wondered if the poor family had a donkey to carry the mother and child. Or would they walk that distance? I thought of the Jerusalem protesters who had trudged to Caesarea. I admired Judaean fortitude.

Two weeks later the family returned. When Tuum and I entered his shop, we were greeted by a changed man. He extended his hand, his face aglow with happiness. "Come in! Come!" He answered my request. "Yes, yes! I will make slippers for you."

I handed him one of Pilate's worn sandals. "Ah – for His Excellency!"

I was surprised that he would even handle any article that belonged to Pilate. "A sturdy foot. . . that one! Well, the slippers will take maybe two . . . three weeks. I have so much work to do." He was apologetic. "I'm sorry that I was gone so long."

"Your daughter. . . how is she?"

"Wonderful! Much better!"

"What happened? Did the rabbi heal her?"

"The Rabbi of Nazareth healed all of us."

"I don't understand . . ."

"Yes, he laid his hands on the baby and our sons. He blessed and played with them. I don't think his followers liked that . . . the time spent with the little ones. But he taught the adults, too. Oh, how he taught us!"

"Then he was a good teacher . . . a good rabbi?"

". . . Perhaps as great as Hillel who taught, what is hateful to thyself do not do to another. That idea was first given to us by Moses in his books. But this Rabbi explained things so well, so clearly . . . Love your enemies. Do good to those who persecute you. Oh, he teaches like no one we've ever heard."

I saw the glow on his face. He talked to us in a friendlier tone – not as despised Romans. Along with the Ten Words as given to Moses, love and virtue seemed the heart of Judaean life.

"I've never thought about loving an enemy," I said. Even if Zio Ammonius wasn't an enemy, I had resented him for many years. What would my life be like if I could love him? Instead I asked, "Who is this new rabbi?"

"Some say the Rabbi from Nazareth is like the expected Messiah!"

I didn't challenge him, because I was unsure about any messiah. Pilate, I knew, would get a hearty laugh from that remark. Each generation produced a messiah. Even Caesar Augustus was called the Messiah. But his years of peace – granted that his peace was an uneasy one – was enforced by Roman troops during his rule. No doubt the long-awaited Judaean messiah from David's line would be quite different from the Roman idea of a strong political leader.

"So, this Galilean messiah loves his enemies? Are you sure he isn't a Zealot, ready to use his sword at any hint of trouble? The Galileans are feisty," I said.

"The greatest commandment is to love Elohim and love your neighbor as yourself. That's what he said."

The Sandal maker appeared different – much more open. I ordered Pilate's slippers. He promised to make the finest pair possible. We, too, left his shop with an inner joy and peace. Whatever happened in Capernaum had changed the relationship of two opposites – the Judaean Sandal maker and me, a Gentile woman – the Prefect's wife.

When Pilate returned, I didn't mention the Sandal maker's experience in Galilee. Afterward, I blamed myself, for I might have saved Pilate some trouble by telling him that not every Galilean hated us – since the Rabbi had advised, *Love your enemies.*

Throughout his tenure, Pilate employed spies. Some had an unsavory past – ruffians who became spies to save their own necks. Highway robbery was always a concern especially at festival times.

A group of Galileans came south for the Feast of Trumpets, also called Feast of the Seventh New Moon. They traveled until sunset, hoping to spend the night in a cave near Jerusalem. Perhaps Pilate's spy wanted to steal their corban for himself. Some caged doves and golden cups were destined for temple sacrifice. Anyway, the spy reported that the travelers were a band of robbers. Pilate ordered a surprise attack. His soldiers killed them all, including the birds.

There was much murmuring, but Caiaphas and the elders didn't send a protest to Roma. After all, the suspects were Galileans, possible trouble-makers. For his own part, Pilate made no apology and remained stone-faced when he heard complaints that he had mingled the blood of the Galileans with their sacrifices.

Chapter XX

In the seventeenth year of Tiberius' reign, couriers brought us disturbing news. The Emperor, now sixty-five, governed from the Isle of Capri. He stayed isolated there with literary Greeks and other flatterers, adding to rumors about his drinking and sexual orgies. In Roma, his trusted appointee, Sejanus, prefect of the Praetorian Guard, governed by following the Emperor's directives. Through the years, Sejanus had eliminated his own personal enemies – even members of Tiberius' family – through false accusations.

Now Tiberius notified the Senate that Gaius, son of his stepdaughter Agrippina, would be his successor at death. Sejanus was furious. He plotted to kill the Emperor and gain the monarchy for himself. Tiberius was warned of Sejanus' plot and notified the Senate. Sejanus was condemned that very night and his accusers strangled him.

When Pilate heard this, his face paled. He had bribed Sejanus for his high position. What if the Emperor found him guilty by association? Tiberius punished his enemies by dragging them through the streets with hooks. The old ruler didn't trust anyone – not even his aides. Only two or three, out of twenty, were still alive. He was shrewd, smart, sour and swift to kill any perceived enemy.

Pilate told me that he must be extremely cautious. He asked himself, "What can I do to remain in Tiberius' favor?"

First, he stopped minting his own personal coins. I kept some as souvenirs in an inlaid box and recalled how Octavianus had stolen coins from me so long ago.

Tuum studied money in her hand and remarked, "How times change! I suppose Pilate's coins are quite worthless now."

Pilate still chafed over his first mistake – the placement of golden shields on the Antonio Fortress in Jerusalem during his first year. This time when Pilate ordered new shields, covered in gold and inscribed with the names of Roman deities, he placed them in our private library in the Mt. Zion palace.

I studied them, huge and poor in artistic design. "Ugh!" I turned away.

Tuum frowned. Quietly, she said, "At least, the shields provided a few metal workers with a job."

When Pilate returned, I said curtly, "I refuse to have those horrid shields in my rooms."

Pilate shrugged and ordered them rehung them in his office area. He was sure the shields would please the Emperor and show that he was a loyal and faithful prefect.

Nothing that happened in the Palace was private. No doubt some servants kept the Temple authorities informed about our activities because later in the month, four Herodian princes appeared, requesting removal of the shields. Both Tetrarchs – Antipas of Galilee and his brother Philip of Batanaea – came with two of their tall Herodian cousins. All wore their royal robes and had a retinue of servants. They were supported by a political party, called the Herodians. It had lost any religious basis, but it was a threat to Judaea's stability.

Pilate argued, "The shields represent the Emperor. His orders are carried out in the palace office. The office is for the empire's business, not religious decisions."

Philip was the most reasonable. He pleaded, "You have no right to defile our father's palace with shields bearing heathen names! Our father was the faithful king of the Jews!"

Pilate stiffened. "Your father called himself King of the Jews. He was not their king. He was an Idumean and granted his title by Roma, not the Judaeans!"

"Don't ignore our traditions!" Antipas snapped.

Pilate was firm, "The shields must stay."

Antipas shook his fist and threatened, "Then, we will write to the Emperor!" He hurried away with the others trailing behind. This seemed to be a final break in any relations between Antipas and Pilate.

"Let's take the shields back to Caesarea. Oh, I'll find someplace for them there," I suggested. Like the dungeon.

Pilate was adamant. "If I say they stay, they stay!"

Nevertheless, the next weeks were uneasy until Tiberius sent his reply – furious in tone and definite in direction. Pilate was to remove the shields and install them in the Temple of Augustus in Caesarea. However, Pilate was not ordered back to Roma in disgrace.

Clodius, Tuum and I all breathed a sigh of relief. Even Pilate relaxed – a little.

When another Passover came, Tuum and I were anxious to return to Jerusalem. As we wandered around, we looked for certain landmarks and people we remembered – the woman in the market who sold oranges, a merchant with spicy eastern perfumes, or the goldsmith from Petra in Arabia. It was hard not to linger in his shop.

One old man always lay by the Beth-Zatha pool near the Sheep Gate. The Judaeans believed that an angel stirred the water (when it was really a spring below). They had a quaint superstition – the first person to bathe after any ripples would be healed. The old man moved so slowly that others crowded ahead of him at that precious moment. I wanted to help him, but it would be unthinkable for a Roman woman to reach down and touch a Judaean man. So, we passed by on the other side of the street.

A young blind man leaned against a wall by the Siloam pool. When Tuum and I walked along, I often dropped a coin in his palm. He was almost like a statue – merely a human signpost. We didn't much think about him.

The next day after Shabbat, a temple priest came to the Palace. He rushed in and demanded to see Pilate. He was very upset, coming at the third hour. Pilate met him on the palace steps, so the priest wouldn't be defiled by entering a Gentile place at Passover time. Tuum and I lingered behind an entrance screen. We heard them quite distinctly.

The priest spoke in a grave voice. "At this most holy season, we have evidence of two men who have broken a sacred law . . . against work on the Shabbat."

Pilate reminded him, "If they've broken your law, then you deal with them. I don't judge temple affairs."

"Such an offense is punishable by death. As temple authorities, we can't order a death sentence. That decision belongs to you . . . to Roma."

"And just what is the charge? "

A sick beggar lay on his pallet by the Sheep Gate pool. A rabbi came along and told him to take up his pallet and walk. On the Shabbat! The old man lugged it into the temple to give thanks! Anunclean man . . . imagine that! This rabbi admits to everything."

"If the man is walking, what's the problem? It means one less beggar."

"This rabbi encouraged him to carry a load on the Shabbat! That's work! Such an act is against Elohim's law!" He tearfully wrung his hands in genuine distress. The priest belonged to the*Sadducees, an aristocratic priestly class who observed the literal meaning of religious law. "How can we remain pure if we ignore holy teaching?"

"You want to be pure?" Pilate laughed. "Why not enjoy life? Live like the Romans! Eat, drink, and be merry!" Then he asked, sharply. "Who was this rabbi?"

"The old man wouldn't tell us at first. Then a Galilean came into the temple. The old man pointed him out as the healing Rabbi from Nazareth."

Pilate gave a hearty laugh. "A Galilean? No educated person comes from there. Do you really believe he heals anyone? He's another ignorant quack. He only helped an old man to his feet." Pilate grew serious. "Be sensible! You may be concerned about religious law but be reasonable. Don't get your elders upset over trivial events. Save your strength for an important criminal act."

"To break any sacred law is an offense against Elohim," the priest said firmly.

"Remember, all of us hold our positions at the Emperor's whim or pleasure. Don't make trouble." Pilate added, "Be wise. Ignore this mistake."

When the priest left, Pilate turned to Clodius who had made notes about the incident. "There's probably no reason to be concerned, yet we can't have the temple authorities too upset. They can quickly create problems, too. We have spies here in Jerusalem. Get some information about this Galilean rabbi. Is he alone . . . or part of a group? Where does he stay? We need to be prepared if he's a troublemaker."

Clodius left. Tuum and I looked at each other. We already knew about the Rabbi from Nazareth.

After breakfast two days later, Clodius brought Pilate his report. "Your Excellency, there's no need to worry about that Galilean rabbi. He is around thirty . . . fairly well-known in the north. A Centurion in Capernaum tells everyone that the Rabbi from Nazareth healed his servant. He has a great deal of faith in him."

"A Centurion? Well, that is a surprise! That man leads some six-hundred soldiers, and he still has faith in a country rabbi?" Pilate laughed. "What else?"

"Our worries are over. The Rabbi has fled to Peraea beyond the Jordan."

Pilate grinned broadly. "Then he's Antipas' problem! Let the old Fox deal with his country practitioner. And tell the temple authorities that their wily rabbi has run away."

Clodius hesitated. "There is one other thing. This rabbi is a cousin of that beheaded prophet . . ."

". . . John, the Baptist?"

"That's the one."

"How strange that he would go to Peraea where that John was killed." He rubbed his chin over another possibility – that the rabbi and Antipas might form an alliance.

I thought, Pilate is wise, strong and so competent. And he is capable – a man of authority. The early problems of the shields and an aqueduct were behind him. He still didn't grasp the Judaeans' full devotion to Yahveh, but he had acted more wisely. Surely, Pilate would serve many more years without too many problems.

I was glad. I loved this harsh land of strange beauty with mountains that seemed a shield against trouble. The valleys bloomed with brilliant wild-flowers. It was always a thrill to see Jerusalem – a city set on a hill which couldn't be hidden. The buildings gleamed like gold in the evening sun. I was confident of our future. At that moment, I felt a great love for Pilate.

In the nineteenth year of Tiberius' reign, no one expected any major trouble in the empire. The fiscal situation appeared to be the most stable in history. Emperor Caesar Augustus had minted more money and produced inflation – believing that spending was the way to prosperity. Emperor Tiberius believed the opposite – that economy was best. New building projects were canceled.

Tiberius' reign meant real peace, no war or conquests for more territory. That was one reason why Pilate had been able to raid the temple treasury for the aqueduct. The empire's treasury held almost three billion copper sesterces. People were confident. Everyone in government felt secure.

Because Emperor Augusutus had established a civil service, Pilate had a salary of a hundred thousand sesterces. A sesterce was equal to four asses in value. One afternoon, Tuum and I amused ourselves by working out the acreage needed if Pilate were paid in asses. Then we figured out how many barns were needed, the number of stalls, and pails of oats. We laughed a great deal. Even Clodius was amused. But Pilate didn't find any humor in it. So, we put away our stylus and tablets and grew serious about whether it would rain.

Pilate's testiness was fueled by rumors from Roma about a financial crisis. He was responsible for fiscal matters. Carefully, he collected taxes and dispensed revenues, so Judaea remained a profitable province for Roma. His records were detailed and accurate.

PROCULA | Marion H. Youngquist

Within two weeks, couriers brought dire news. It was true – there was a great panic in Roma. No one understood how it was possible with our banking system – the finest in the world. Banks had multi-functions: checking accounts and interest-bearing deposits, bills of exchange and traveler notes, investments and loans, especially money for partnerships. Even real estate was managed, bought and sold through banks. Surely, the great financial firms were safe – but not from the government.

For some time, the Senate had been concerned that too much capital was going to eastern trading centers for luxuries. So, it decreed that a high percentage of every Senator's salary had to be invested in Roman land. When Senator Publius Spinther, who had attended our wedding, announced that he would withdraw thirty million sesterces from the Balbus and Ollius bank, the great house announced bankruptcy. Would others follow?

I saw Pilate's troubled brow. In private, he held me close and said, "Procula, we must be strong. Our own situation is difficult. Many fortunes are gone."

I felt a chill. Some of my dowry was left in the Balbus and Ollius bank. Had Lucius already saved it? I was glad for the property that I owned in AEgyptus.

I hugged him. "Your salary? Surely, the government will pay all the salaries."

"Oh yes! Tiberius has suspended the land-investment act and has sent a hundred million sesterces to the banks for loans without interest in real-estate transactions. Maybe the lower interest rates will aid in recovery. Who knows?"

We were both quiet until Pilate said, "The tax-collectors must be very diligent this year. We must add some new taxes."

I wondered who and what else could be taxed. Only rabbis were exempt.

Collectors were important because there were taxes on everything: income, food, land taxes based on harvest, on goods, purchase taxes, import and export fees, custom charges, road and bridge tolls. The poll tax, at census time, was sent directly to Roma. Another complication was the purchase of a province by a huge partnership in Roma and the dispute over the revenues from that area directed by the partnership.

It was Cicero, the great orator and man of letters, who said *vectugulia nervos esse re i publicae* –meaning taxes are essential to the strength of the Republic.

When the tax men made their rounds, they added fees for themselves and the rulers. Pilate counted on a good stipend. And there was always *unguentaria* – ointment money – to grease the palm of an official. The Romans liked to hire capable Judaeans to collect from their own people, because a collector knew his neighbors and could assess them fairly.

Emperor Tiberius had advised his provincial governors to be good shepherds – shear, but don't fleece the sheep.

Along with the Panic, another event unsettled Pilate. The tax collector in Jericho resigned. Pilate immediately blamed robbery or intimidation by thieves during tax time. The Jericho road, which descended so steeply, was often terrorized by ruffians.

"No," Clodius reported, laughing. "It seems he's gone religious!"

"Losing Zaccheus is no laughing matter," Pilate snapped. "He's one of the best. He always collects taxes on time, and with a generous cut for me. There's never been a mistake when he's been audited. I don't understand this at all!"

"It has something to do with some rabbi's new teaching."

Pilate signed a paper and handed it to Clodius. "Here's an order. Bring him to me. I want to hear his story. He can't resign on such a flimsy excuse. Religion, indeed!"

So, the next day, Zaccheus stood before Pilate. Again, Tuum and I were so curious that we peeked from the anteroom. Zaccheus was a short swarthy man with a round face and intelligent eyes. He surveyed the room, appraising the furnishings and Pilate's attitude. He knew the value of everything. Nothing could escape his piercing glance.

Pilate went through the formalities quickly. "Just why are you leaving the Emperor's service? You've been the tax collector during my seven years as prefect."

Zaccheus nodded, "Oh yes! And three years before that under Valerius Gratus." He hesitated, searching for the right words. "It's just that my life has changed." His smile was warm and confident – much like that of the Sandal maker. He was at ease, even facing Pilate who represented the power of Roma. "I met the Rabbi from Nazareth . . ."

"That little town?" Pilate laughed. "Can anything good come out of Nazareth?"

"He made me realize that there is more to life than money."

"Like what?" Pilate said dryly. "You've never complained before."

". . . Like family . . . friends . . . and Elohim."

"I believe that a family, and friends . . . and even your god Yahveh . . . like money in the bank. The temple authorities have never refused corban!"

"Perhaps so, but money was too important to me." Zaccheus reflected a bit. "Looking back on how it happened, I believe this rabbi is a prophet, sent by Elohim to call me . . . us . . . to repentance . . . to turn away from our old ways and to fully live!"

"And just how did you meet this . . . this prophet?"

118

PROCULA | Marion H. Youngquist

"That's the most amazing part of all! He came walking down the Jericho road. I'm so short that I climbed up in a sycamore tree to see him. There was a crowd of travelers with him. As he came by the tree, he glanced up and saw me. Maybe someone whispered to shun me, because I was a tax collector."

"An excellent one! One that the Emperor appreciates . . .," Pilate reminded him.

"Instead, the Rabbi called me to come down. Then he asked if he might rest awhile at my house! Think of that . . . at my house . . . a tax-collector's house!"

"And why not? You're a very rich man. Have I ever argued with you about your percentage? You and I have understood each other very well," Pilate said. "You have good reason to feel proud of what you have accomplished."

Zaccheus ignored him. "Well . . . I had the servants fix a small feast and several of my friends came. The news traveled fast . . . that he was eating with me . . . a publicanus . . . almost a farmer of taxes. . . and with my friends. I know that I'm criticized as a hypocrite . . . collecting taxes one day and praying, the next."

"That's rather harsh. You attend the synagogue. You say your prayers and give your offerings. You're as righteous as any Pharisee."

"I considered myself a good person," Zaccheus continued. "Then the Rabbi told us a story about a Pharisee and a publicanus . . . similar to me. The Rabbi said,

> Two men went into the Temple to pray. One was a
> Pharisee and one, a publicanus. In his prayer, the
> Pharisee reminded Elohim of his own holiness. But
> the publicanus . . . like me . . .stood just inside the
> door and prayed for Elohim to be merciful because he
> was a sinner! And Elohim accepted his prayer
> because he was humble.

I tell you that story changed my life! I realized that for all my riches and goodness, I was really selfish. I needed the mercy of Elohim. I knew deep down that I was missing a real relationship with Elohim."

Pilate turned away, "If your Yahveh shows mercy, he's more powerful than any I know. We Romans barter with the gods all the time." He could have added, what good does bargaining do?

Zaccheus smiled, "The Rabbi talked until midnight. He was impressive and inspiring. I realized that Elohim is not only great and good as the

119

praise-songs say, but he cares for each one of us. He said that even the hairs on our head are numbered . . ."

Pilate patted his thinning hair. "Really? He won't spend much time on me!"

Zaccheus took a deep breath and said, "I struggled over what the Rabbi had said. When I saw the Rabbi the next day, I told him that I would give half my wealth to the poor. Also, to those I've defrauded, I'll return four times their money. And each day, I'll confess my sins and repent."

Pilate looked stunned, "You'll be penniless. You can't afford to do all of that!"

Zaccheus said quietly, "I can't afford not to do it. I am at peace with Elohim, my neighbors, and myself." The Rabbi said, "*For what does it profit a man to gain the whole world and forfeit his life?*" He added softly, ". . . or his soul?"

At the word *soul,* Pilate hardened his tone, "Your wife and family? They can't be happy about this change."

Zaccheus admitted, "No, you're right. It is a shock. But the Rabbi predicted that not everyone will believe him. He said some families will quarrel over his teachings."

"And you find comfort in making trouble for your own sons? How will you live?"

"We still have our house. Perhaps we will turn it into an inn. A good one is needed in Jericho." Then he added, "It won't hurt my sons to learn to work together and earn their own way." He slumped in his chair with momentary sadness. "The youngest already wants his inheritance so that he can live in Caesarea or go to Roma." He looked away.

"Evidently, I can't persuade you otherwise," Pilate frowned. "I don't understand you, but there are others who want your position." Pilate needled him. "Your successor can start with you when he makes his rounds to collect taxes."

"Yes, I know," Zaccheus nodded. "But the Rabbi tells us to take up our cross and follow him."

"Cross? We Romans crucify those who are criminals . . . on a cross. That's a strange invitation to your new life."

"Yes, but the Rabbi promised *those who find their life will lose it, and those who lose their life for my sake will find it.*"

Pilate's jaw tightened. "It sounds like a lot of double-talk . . . losing and finding! Get out! Don't ever ask for any favor!" He turned his back.

Zaccheus stopped at the door, "I will pray for you, Your Excellency."

Pilate waved him away. "Save your prayers for yourself! Why would I need any of your prayers?"

The Judaeans religious fervor continued to puzzle Pilate. Their devotion completely mystified him. He couldn't understand why they couldn't be practical in daily affairs and save their piety for Shabbat.

Tuum and I crept back to our quarters. We didn't speak for a while. Finally, Tuum said, "I wish I could meet the Rabbi from Nazareth."

I admitted, "So do I!"

News of Roma's failed banks worried Pilate. Other dire reports followed. An Alexandrian firm, Seuthes and Sons, closed because three ships, carrying spices, were lost in a storm. Banks in Lyons, Carthage, Corinth and Byzantium also closed. Deep lines spread across Pilate's brow and his temples seemed grayer. He and his staff worked into the night on financial reports, a major function for a prefect.

I remembered the lines from Ovid –

How little you know of the age you live in, if you fancy that honey is sweeter than cash in hand.

I thought of Zio Ammonius and his palatial homes. He selected and embraced his Epicurean delights – rich food, soft togas, painted scenes on walls, woven hangings and fine wines – with such finesse. Things. How could he live with anything less?

Then, a difficult letter arrived from Lucius:

To Procula, esteemed wife of Pontius Pilate, Prefect of Judaea –

I regret that I must send you sad news. Your Zio Ammonius fell from his balcony at Villa Mirabele-By-The-Sea two weeks ago. We do not know what happened as he was alone. His health had failed with the recent bank closures.

Domum Fontana has been sold. Julius is still at Villa Fortunata.

My house and garden await me in Alexandria. Your property in Alexandria has proved a sound investment for you. Other money was transferred months ago to Alexandria, so you have not suffered in the great financial panic.

My hair has turned almost white. Ever your friend, Lucius.

Both Tuum and I were equally silent. I felt a terrible guilt that I had never made peace with Zio Ammonius, especially at our farewell. My resentment over his dictates weighed heavily on me. He took me from Arretium, arranged an awful marriage to his son, and invested my dowry. It was as if he had stolen my life. And yet – for my own peace of mind – could I continue to bear that grudge? After all, Domum Fontana was my home. I met Pilate there and married him. I came to Judaea with an envied position as the Prefect's wife. Still, I couldn't forget my harsh words when I left Zio Ammonius.

Although I bore sadness and regret with a certain Stoic detachment, I began to evaluate my own life – both my pride and poverty of spirit. I did believe all living things were partially divine. I accepted most disappointments without emotion. However, a vague emptiness troubled me. Stoicism didn't help. There had to be something more.

Chapter XXI

Despite their beautiful temples, the variety of Roman and Greek gods in Caesarea were meaningless. Pilate observed religious ceremonies on behalf of the Emperor, although his real belief was in the strength and power of the state. I found nothing in the old gods or the state to nourish my spirit.

I thought of the radiant joy that both the Sandal maker and Zaccheus had expressed. It was obvious that their lives were centered in a deep commitment to Yahveh. I envied their confidence and hope. Yahveh seemed to be a living presence in every moment of every day. I needed that presence. I was also impressed with their concern for their neighbors – the good deeds that they did for others. I needed to love others more. Maybe, someday, I could even love the memory of Zio Ammonius. I decided to pursue a long-felt interest in Judaism.

I knew the Sandal maker was a Hellenized Jew, comfortable with both Greek and Judaic culture. He was a very faithful Judaean, who always closed his shop when the first star shone on Shabbat Eve. He observed all holy days and festivals, even when trading ships docked, and sales might be plentiful.

Tuum and I stopped in his shop.

"I would like to know more about your faith," I said. "Could I hire your son Aaron to teach me Hebrew, so I could read the Torah, too?"

Did he look at me with questioning eyes – can she master the curved markings of our difficult alphabet? No. Instead, he said, "That would be good . . . very good. I want him to be a Scribe someday. He will teach you, and even interpret and copy our sacred scripture. Aaron does very well in our synagogue and school," he added proudly.

So, on a midweek afternoon, Tuum and I listened while Aaron, read a passage from the prophet Isaiah:

Thus, says Adonai: Maintain justice, and do what is right, for soon my salvation will come, and my deliverance will be revealed.

Blessed are those who do this, and the son of man who holds it fast, who keeps the Shabbat, not profaning it, and keeps his hand from doing evil . .
.

When he read on, I listened intently for the verses seemed to speak directly to me:

. . . And the foreigners who join themselves to Adonai, to minister to him, to love the name of Adonai, and to be his servants, all who keep the Shabbat, and do not profane it, and hold fast my covenant – these I will bring to my holy mountain, and make them joyful in my house of prayer; their burnt offerings and their sacrifices will be accepted on my altar; for my house shall be called a house of prayer for all peoples.

I found myself drawn to these words. Would Yahveh accept me – a Gentile woman – on His holy mountain and in His house of prayer? Was His house really for all peoples?

Because Aaron impressed on me that the Temple was at the heart of Jewish faith, I wanted to return to Jerusalem for the Feast of Dedication that winter. It was a joyous time. The Judaean homes and the Temple were especially festive with lights. People carried palm branches and sang the Hallel. Their celebration always marked the end of a terrible persecution two centuries ago.

We remained in Jerusalem to celebrate the Roman Saturnalia, too. That time meant extra work for Tuum and me. We found suitable holiday presents for the staff – jars of ointments, perfumes, boxes of dried fruits, oil lamps and bottles of wine. Suddenly, Saturnalia seemed a celebration without substance. It didn't have a deeper meaning like the Feast of Dedication. My finest jewels lacked the brightness of blessed candlelight.

However, practical matters demanded my attention. At the end of the year, there were accounts to balance, inventories, new supplies, and a wine cellar to stock. My years at Domum Fontana and in the country under Zia

Terentia's instruction left me capable and efficient. Pilate said that the palaces ran more smoothly when I supervised the steward and servants. He needed my services because his staff was small – an interpreter, a clerk, his personal groom, a military captain and two messengers. Some guards held multiple roles as secretaries, accountants or spies.

As I dropped a requisition in Pilate's office, Caiaphas and two leaders of the Sanhedrin, arrived. Pilate expected it was a courtesy call – a greetings of the season. I left but lingered in an anteroom where I could glimpse and hear the verbal sparring.

Caiaphas was tall or appeared so in his robe and long cloak. He had a prominent hawk-nose and hazel eyes that avoided a direct gaze. It was unusual that he would come. Usually, a lesser priest delivered his messages. His tightened jaw expressed his concern. His resonant voice boomed out – a priestly tone from years of chanting.

Two men accompanied him – Nicodemus, the rich man who had accompanied Caiaphas about the aqueduct project, and Jakob, who sold litters and wagons. Both were Pharisees and members of the Sanhedrin.

Caiaphas phrased his words carefully, "I wanted to see you before anyone else reported the . . . the . . . small upset in the Temple this morning. It concerns us. We wanted you to know of it."

Pilate stiffened. A small upset wouldn't cause Caiaphas to make this call.

"It seems that the Rabbi from Nazareth has been in Jerusalem for the Feast of Dedication. He argued with some very learned scholars. He, again. . . so I hear. . . claimed that Elohim is his father, and that his followers will have eternal life! That is against all sacred teaching!"

Eternal life? Pilate put his hand over his mouth to suppress a laugh.

I was instantly alert. I wanted to hear more. I wondered if the Rabbi from Nazareth were a Pharisee. That sect believed in resurrection as well as a strict interpretation of both oral and written laws, especially those relating to cleanliness and uncleanliness. There were only about six thousand *Pharisees, but they were intelligent and influential. Dialog seemed to be their favorite activity – answering a question with another question.

Caiaphas continued, "This is blasphemous, of course, to us . . . the true sons of Abraham. The crowd picked up some rocks and wanted to stone him."

Jakob interrupted, ". . . Well, not everyone. I confronted the Rabbi from Nazareth about the blasphemy and he said,

If you don't believe me, believe the good works that came from our Father.

For which one of the healing's will you stone me?"

Jakob shook his head sadly, "He can't stay out of trouble if he talks like that!"

Caiaphas frowned, "Evidently, he just walked away while the others argued about which offense was greatest . . . his claim that Elohim is our father or healing on Shabbat." He paused, "Understand . . . I feel responsible for sacred teachings and pious lives here in Jerusalem."

"This seems a rather minor quarrel over words . . ." Pilate said. "You allow many things to be discussed . . . a simple idea of . . ."

". . . Not to us!" Caiaphas answered. "But there really is more. From what others say, this rabbi makes fantastic claims about some kingdom. . . his or his . . . his father's." He almost choked on the words. "I believe he's a Zealot at heart. He says he comes not to bring peace, but a sword! Does he intend to lead an insurrection? I think so!"

When Caiaphas mentioned kingdom and insurrection, Pilate lifted his eyebrows, alert to all the nuances. Did the Rabbi and Antipas support each other in a plan to conquer Judaea?

Nicodemus interrupted, "The Rabbi really meant a heavenly kingdom . . ."

Was Nicodemus sympathetic to the upstart rabbi? I wanted to ask. But, as a Gentile woman, I must remain unseen and silent.

". . . While he claims to be a Galilean," Caiaphas continued, "some believe the Rabbi may be a Samaritan. He tells a story about a good Samaritan. But we know that the Samaritans are not true followers of Elohim. Since Samaritis is under your direct jurisdiction, you must stop him to keep the peace."

Pilate sighed. He knew about the quarrels between Samaritis and Judaea over holy land. The Samaritans claimed that Abraham's altar site for slaying Isaac was on their Mt. Gerizim. They also claimed to have the oldest copy of the Torah. In the Torah, Moses clearly stated and commanded that any blessings of the Law be proclaimed from Gerizim, while curses should proceed from the opposite mountain called Ebal. There were rumors that Moses had buried some golden artifacts on Mt. Gerizim. For the Samaritans, this made their hilltop more sacred than Mt. Zion in Jerusalem.

To the Judaeans, Samaritis was populated by heathens – descendants of a mixed race after centuries of war and intermarriage. They denied the Samaritan claims of owning the oldest Pentateuch, or of fully observing the Law. Although the Samaritans still practiced circumcision, the Judaeans found them impure because they mixed in idol worship with their temple rites. The rivalry was so intense that Pilate kept his Samaritis-born troops out of Jerusalem to prevent an unprovoked attack on the Judaeans.

Jakob hesitated, "It is reported that the Rabbi is honored in Samaritis. Some woman claims that he's changed her life. He met her at the town well

and told her that he would give her living water. . . whatever that means."
He shook his head. "The Rabbi stayed there for two days! He has some
local followers now . . . that's for sure."

Caiaphas' voice shook, "Do you need more proof? That man is as
unclean as the Samaritans! He'll raise an army against us!"

Pilate considered everything. "Well, if this rabbi creates any trouble or
raises an army of his own, we'll deal with him swiftly. We must keep peace
at all costs."

Pilate emphasized his own authority to the Sanhedrin group. Uprisings
were a worry because his military strength was rather thin. The empire's
power came from a history of swift action by well-prepared Roman militia.
Every province feared quick reprisals. Vertical posts stood ready for prisoners carrying their crossbeams for crucifixion.

Caiaphas was upset. "Well, this rabbi is a wily one. He cleverly maneu-
vers any argument. The Pharisees asked him if it was lawful to pay the
Emperor's tax. He took a silver coin and said, pay to Caesar that which is
Caesar's and to Elohim whatever belongs to him."

Pilate thought about the worsening financial crisis. A faint smile crossed
his face. At least the Rabbi from Nazareth didn't tell his listeners to quit
paying taxes.

After the angry group left, Pilate studied the large regional map against
the north wall. I walked up behind Clodius and Fabius, the commander
who assisted Pilate in military maneuvers.

"Something may be afoot," Pilate mused. "If there's trouble in Samaritis,
we'll have to stop it immediately. Otherwise, Antipas can claim that he will
govern better . . . and by inherited right! Even with his divided territory, he
surrounds Judaea. Some Senators in Roma might persuade Tiberius that a
restored Herodian province would be easier to manage than one split into
three parts . . . and not as costly."

Clodius observed, "Then Antipas will ask to be crowned a king, like his
father."

"Any king of Judaea will wear an uneasy crown," Pilate remarked.

"We'll have a king soon!" Fabius laughed. "The soldiers will draw lots
tonight to choose a King of Saturnalia. That means a rich robe, rich food,
and plenty of women for thirty days! And his friends will line up to see him
stagger back to his barracks."

"That's better than that game Basilinda that the soldiers play," Clodius
grimaced. "The winner picks a prisoner as king . . . robes him in an old army
blanket and crowns him with a thorny wreath. Everyone salutes him before
he's crucified."

"How horrible," I murmured.

Pilate replied firmly, "It's better that some prisoners are executed, if it means peace can be maintained." He turned away from the map. "We'll watch the situation in Samaritis closely."

Pilate had noted Caiaphas' concern over the Rabbi from Nazareth or Galilee or Samaritis – or wherever he came from. However, Pilate didn't seem worried.

Whenever we were in Jerusalem, Tuum and I blended into the crowd. We dressed as local women with cotton tunics underneath rough linen robes, long enough to reach our feet. Veils were important, and we covered our faces. We walked beside each other, rather than Tuum following me as a devoted slave. We might have been neighbors going to market. No one realized we were Romans.

It was Tuum who pointed out that the young blind man was gone from his spot at the pool of Siloam. I dropped two bronze coins into a nearby beggar's outstretched hand – enough for a public bath.

Tuum asked him, "The young blind man who was here . . . is he ill or has he moved away?"

"No!" said the beggar. "He was healed by the Rabbi from Nazareth. That's caused such a stir! The Pharisees didn't believe that he was cured, so they questioned his parents rather harshly . . . to see if they lied about his sight."

Was Nicodemus among the questioners? What would he make of this unusual story? If he had his sight, what did it matter how he was healed?

"His parents sent the authorities back to their son. And the son said, Elohim listens to those who do his will. I don't know if the rabbi is a sinner . . . all I know is that once I was blind, and now I see. If this man were not from Elohim, he could do nothing."

The beggar chuckled, "I tell you, that upset the temple crowd! The young man has left town and so has the Rabbi."

Tuum and I read each other's thoughts. It was good that the young man gained his sight, but we wondered where he'd gone. Even more, we were disappointed that the Rabbi from Nazareth had left Jerusalem again. Perhaps we would never see him. Who was he really? An itinerant preacher? A faith healer? A Zealot?

Or something more?

When we returned to Caesarea, we resumed our studies with Aaron. He read the scrolls and explained so much. We discovered how Yahveh had led his people through the centuries. It was an exciting history. A special

PROCULA | Marion H. Youngquist

covenant, made with Abraham, continued to this day. Both Tuum and I looked forward to each Tuesday. The Genesis story of Creation became my favorite. After Aaron left, Tuum and I talked about all we'd heard.

I mulled over how the great Yahveh breathed his spirit into Adam. "That is such a beautiful story," I said.

Tuum's eyes sparkled with good humor. "Oh, Adam was created after all the animals were made. It's too bad that Yahveh didn't give him a tail for swatting flies!"

I caught her playfulness. "If we had fur like the leopards, we wouldn't need a warm robe in winter!"

"If we had legs like frogs, we could really jump. That would be fun, especially if we were children!"

". . . And people worry so much, maybe we were given too many brains."

Tuum and I laughed out loud. Pilate wanted to know what was so funny, so we told him. He shrugged, "Enjoy the Torah, if you care to dabble with it. I have no time for endless prayers. I find reading about the great men of history . . . Julius Caesar or Pompey or Augustus . . . more inspiring."

Tuum spoke up. "Those men are all dead! Yahveh's people are very much alive!"

Pilate stopped and looked at her as if he'd heard surprising news. "Well, so be it!" He left the room with a troubled scowl.

Through Esther, we joined a small group of both Hellenized Jews and Romans who gathered weekly to study the Torah. Her husband, Cornelius, was the Roman Centurion stationed with the Italian Guard. When we first met, we found something in common – he was from Genua, a port city northwest of Arretium.

Pilate wasn't pleased with my increasing need for spiritual nourishment. Yet, he knew that some Judaeans might be more sympathetic to him, if it were known that he had a wife who was interested in their religion. "Why do you discuss an unseen god when Roman and Greek gods were satisfactory for our ancestors? Is Cornelius only anxious to have you listen to scripture because of your soul?"

Tuum, amused, guessed he was irritated because Cornelius was only forty, and very good-looking with a ruddy complexion and steel-blue eyes.

"Bibi – he's jealous!" she whispered, laughing.

That surprised me, but I knew Pilate's first marriage failed because of his wife's infidelity. Perhaps he would never fully trust anyone again – even me.

"We've known Esther and Cornelius since we arrived over five years ago. She helped me so much. Our study group includes a variety of people . . . Romans, Greeks, an Idumean . . . even their slaves."

129

"Questions and more questions! It's sure to be noisy. How can your Yahveh hear any prayers with all the confusion? Procula, believe if you must, but promise not to get too full of prayers and good works. I don't want you to change," Pilate added.

I couldn't promise that. As scriptures were read, I questioned many things in my mind. Among the Judaeans, searching questions were asked. At our gatherings, I found the various viewpoints stimulating. Once when the group discussed Abraham, I found the courage to offer an idea.

"I like a special passage in Genesis . . .I will multiply your descendants like stars of heaven and will give to your descendants all these lands; and by your descendants all the nations of the earth shall bless themselves. That scripture is so beautiful to me because through you, I will be blessed also." Maybe even Pilate will be blessed someday, too, I thought, but now I need reassurance of a relationship with Yahveh.

The others listened respectfully. I hoped they accepted me because I was eager to learn and intelligent – not because I was the Prefect's wife. It was a new and unusual experience for me to be a Gentile woman studying with learned Judaeans.

Then Aaron recited the prayer, being used by followers of the Rabbi from Nazareth:

> "Our Father in heaven, hallowed be your name,
> your kingdom come, your will be done on earth
> as it is in heaven. Give us today our daily bread.
>
> Forgive us our sins as we forgive those who sin
> against us. Save us from the time of trial and
> deliver us from evil."

Someone asked, "Do we dare call Elohim Father?"

Reaction spread through the room – blasphemy, a break with tradition, against the writings of Moses, so human and ordinary – as the voices continued.

Aaron interrupted, "In the praise songs, there are these words,

> Sing to Adonai sing praises to his name; lift up a
> song to him who rides upon the clouds; his name is
> Adonai, exult before him!
> Father of the fatherless and protector of widows
> is Adonai in his holy habitation."

Our group was silent while it considered the ancient song.

Then, I spoke up – a bit loudly – and people hushed. "It warms my heart to call Yahveh Father. Our Roman gods never touched my life. They were remote, angry and mercurial. I was always afraid and ready to bargain. If Yahveh is my heavenly Father, then he is near and caring and ever-watchful."

A few nodded in agreement and added qualities like forgiving and provider. Our discussion drifted to other words in the Rabbi's prayer – to save us from the time of trial. Did a trial mean something personal like a prolonged illness? Was slavery and the exodus from Egypt a necessary trial to unite a people? At the word slavery, I glanced at Tuum. She stood in the doorway with other slaves, silent and listening raptly to the discussion. Was being bound to me – always answering my command – a trial for her? I turned away, afraid that I might discover a truth that I didn't want to face. Perhaps to believe in Yahveh meant changes I hadn't anticipated. Faith certainly raised difficult questions.

Cornelius was asked how he could be both a Roman Centurion and a follower of Yahveh, too, since soldiers sometimes had to kill others.

He answered slowly. "We're at peace now. We must keep the peace. The army only executes those Judaeans guilty of murder and crimes against the state. I'm not involved in any crucifixions. That would be hard for me. I am a peacekeeper."

One man spit out, "Send any guilty prisoner to Roma . . . or the lions. We don't need Roman justice here. We don't need any peacekeepers! Leave us alone! Then we could live in peace and freedom!"

"I hear Bar-Abbas is jailed in Jerusalem. He ought to be crucified for all the robberies and murders by his mob," suggested another.

". . . But if innocent people are killed, that is against Elohim's will." Aaron said. "We must remember the Ten Words. The Fifth word says, Thou shall not kill."

An old man offered, "It can't happen. We have the courts and judges . . ."

"Only the Romans and our prefect, Pontius Pilate, can order a death sentence," added another.

Both approval and questioning look met my glance. Quickly, I looked away.

The Goldsmith stood up, "We, as Judaeans, must remember crucifixion is a terrible thing. It is the ultimate sign that Elohim has abandoned us. If I suffer and die in prison, if I die of thirst in the desert, if I'm found frozen wrapped in my cloak against the cold . . . in these and any other ways . . . Elohim will find me and bless me forever. But not if I'm crucified! That means Elohim has cast me away forever!"

We were all silenced by his outburst.

That night I asked Pilate if he'd ever sentenced an innocent man to be crucified.

"Don't worry your pretty head. It's no concern of yours." he shrugged.

The next day, Tuum was unusually silent. I asked if she were feeling ill.

"Oh, no, Bibi. I am thinking about what you said last night . . . about Yahveh being your Father. Is he my Father, too?"

I thought a moment. Tuum had no knowledge of any father, since she had been birthed in Roma's back alleys. Surely, the great Yahveh, as father, would mean much to her. "Why, yes, Tuum, of course . . . Yahveh is your father, too."

She brightened, "Then, if Yahveh is your father, and Yahveh is my father – then that makes us sisters. Doesn't it?"

I was silent, taken aback by her logic. "Yes, I guess it does."

"Then we will always be together . . . like a real family . . . won't we?" She started to brush my hair. "I always wanted a sister, didn't you?"

Long ago, I had a sister – only for a brief hour. Then she was placed in a burial cave. The loss of both my mother and baby sister, as well as my father, would always remain. However, my heart could open wide enough for another sister. Many times, Tuum and I thought alike because we shared so much. She became my slave when I was about fourteen and she was, maybe, ten. That was almost two decades ago.

"Yes. Tuum, Yahveh has made us sisters. I think we should have the Goldsmith make us matching bracelets, so we never forget who we are."

She insisted, "Bibi, I will still be your slave – but I will be your sister, too."

Perhaps, she could live with the contradiction, but I knew that I could never really own her again.

"No, Tuum. We are sisters. You are free."

Chapter XXII

I didn't tell Pilate that Tuum and I had become sisters, so now he was her brother-in-law. He wouldn't have seen the humor – or truth – in it. Pilate was focused on his own work. Neither would he understand why Tuum and I looked forward to our seventh Passover in Jerusalem. Seven was a holy number in Jewish lore. Yahveh created the world in six days and rested on the seventh. The golden menorah lamp stands in the temple had seven wicks. The Rabbi from Nazareth taught that forgiveness demanded forgiving seventy-times seven. Seven meant completeness.

Pilate anticipated the seventh Passover as one of order and peace. I was sure that Passover would be a blessed time, even if Pilate didn't worship or pray to Yahveh. Daily Tuum and I prayed privately together to Yahveh and memorized praise-songs.

Pilate left the Samaritan Cohort in Caesarea to avoid conflict with the Judaeans. He chose his best soldiers – the Italian Cohort – to accompany us. This meant that Cornelius was the leader with six hundred cavalry riders acting as guards and peacekeepers.

Our procession was impressive – fine strong horses and uniformed riders with their flashing helmets and gear. Pilate knew mounted soldiers controlled a crowd quicker than foot soldiers. He was prepared for any possible riot.

"Cornelius is an excellent commander," Pilate grudgingly admitted, "of highest ability. He won't have time to read the Torah during Passover. No, everyone is on alert!"

Tuum lowered her glance, lest she burst out laughing at Pilate's pointed remark. He was wary of the interest in Judaism that Cornelius and I shared. He bought me a sapphire ring – a symbol of purity. Often, I wore my emerald necklace – a mark of my faithfulness.

We arrived a week early. The trees had leafed out and red tulips from the Parthian traders were already in bloom. It seemed that nothing could go wrong.

Pilate's spies reported things were quiet in Samaritis. This Passover would remain a time of blessed joy, reflection and prayer. Pilate's spies also reported that the Rabbi from Nazareth had been in heated arguments with the Pharisees. Or were they again – question after question? However, the Rabbi and his followers left each evening to stay in Bethany.

All things seemed quiet.

On the first day of the week, Tuum and I slipped away to enjoy the countryside. This time we rode in a smaller carriage pulled by two draft horses. A young soldier paced them slowly on the well-built road which was wide enough to keep troops, traders and couriers moving. Cornelius sent four cavalries with us – two in front and two in the back – as guards.

At my request, the soldier led us through the east gate, across the Kidron Valley toward Bethany, a village located two miles away. We enjoyed the brilliant hillsides, so scenic with emerging blooms – wild red geranium, yellow crocus and blue lupine. Even distant mountains gleamed like gold. It was breath-taking We were happy.

We'd traveled a furlong when Tuum pointed out, "Look, Bibi! The people want to welcome us . . . You!"

It was true. Small groups along the road waved palm branches and smiled.

I looked back and realized that a few men clenched their raised fists in anger at our Roman carriage and the cavalry riders.

"No, Tuum, this celebration isn't for us. Maybe, it's a traditional rite before Passover begins."

Of course, there were other travelers on the road. Most were pilgrims going toward Jerusalem for Passover, so the road was crowded. We jostled along. I motioned Stop! to the lead soldier, so we could rest in a grove of tamarisk trees, covered with pink blooms. Tuum and I quenched our thirst with oranges. We were puzzled when the nearby crowd grew noisier. We heard distant singing. The cavalry guards mounted their horses, alert for any danger. The captain suggested that we leave.

"But the crowd isn't looking at us," Tuum pointed out. "Someone's coming."

It was true. Along with other pilgrims, a man rode along, seated on a donkey. We knew he was important, because other men walked beside the animal to create a physical barrier. The crowd burst out with shouts of *Hosanna! Blessed is he who comes in the name of Elohim! Peace in heaven and glory in the highest!"* Some clapped. Some cried. His protectors quickly pushed aside anyone who reached out to touch him.

Tuum asked, "Who is he?"

Neither our driver nor the guards knew.

I studied the donkey rider as he passed by. He gazed over the throng with a pensive look. Occasionally, he smiled and nodded. Then he retreated into himself – a man of contemplation, wary of this enthusiastic reception. He was short, like Zaccheus, but with a leaner, sinewy look of someone who usually walked the paved roads instead of riding. His skin was leathery from sun and wind – perhaps he worked outdoors. His robe was that of a simple peasant. Surely, he was poor if he rode a donkey.

Why was the crowd shouting unless this was a reenactment of some event in Judaean history? Maybe the rider represented Judas Maccabeus or King David from ancient times. These country pilgrims fell in behind him and headed to Jerusalem like a great parade.

To avoid more people, the captain planned to go on to Bethany, circle south to Bethphage and then return to Jerusalem. Quickly, I sent a guard to ask the rider's name.

He said, "The man is the Rabbi from Nazareth."

Tuum and I were stunned. Inside the carriage, our confusion continued.

"How can the temple priests get so upset?" Tuum wondered. "He's just a country rabbi." Disappointed, she added, "He looks so ordinary."

Then I remembered the crowds. Maybe he was more than a teacher or healer. A prophet? A seer? Who was this Rabbi from Nazareth?

Arriving at the palace, we were excited to tell Pilate that we had, at last, seen the controversial rabbi. He was unimpressed. His spies had already reported that the Rabbi from Nazareth was riding on a donkey, he laughed, to come to Jerusalem for Passover.

"Oh, Master," Tuum exclaimed, "it was wonderful. People were singing . . ." She clapped her hands like she was an eyewitness to a special event.

". . . And he's quite ordinary. He reminds me of Zaccheus," I added. I was wrong to mention his former tax-collector for Pilate frowned. Then I realized that he wasn't concerned about Zaccheus or the Rabbi.

"Did Cornelius go with you?" he asked.

Tuum suppressed a giggle. I was restrained and said, "No, he sent four cavalry guards . . . one a captain . . . and a lead pacer. I don't know their names or the horses."

"Well, you were protected. That's the most important thing. Anything else of interest?"

Tuum waited for me to tell more about the shouting crowds and waving palm branches.

Instead, I said, "The hillsides were filled with wildflowers . . . very beautiful. Tuum, I want to freshen up before the meal. My bath is waiting."

We left the room. Would we ever see the Rabbi from Nazareth again?

Often Tuum and I left the palace in the early morning. Pilate never approved of our private excursions. We had a secret signal between us when we wanted to leave. One of us would quickly circle her face and pull her hand across her mouth, in a casual gesture. It really meant, "Let's put on our native outfits and get out of here."

We liked to see Jerusalem come alive. That day we headed for the Fish Gate – a distance – to enjoy fresh crusty rolls from a Syrian baker. A favorite silk merchant had a stall at Fishgate square – an open space for traders. The area was also available if troops had to defend the city in an assault. Farmers arrived early, so we did too. Although trades people supplied the palace with everything, we liked to shop. We bought our own treats, like sticky honey-and-nut triangles, and stuffed dates with almonds.

As we passed the Antonio Fortress where troops were stationed, we heard a great noise. We jumped back as the troops rushed down the street in double time, their swords drawn and shields ready. Both Tuum and I quickly returned to the palace, aware that trouble had erupted somewhere.

I expected another lecture if Pilate discovered we were outside the palace during a riot. When we arrived breathless, the sentries said that a Temple priest demanded to see Pilate. So Tuum and I crept down a hallway and stood behind the high screen with its damask hangings. We heard his complaint, made in behalf of Caiaphas.

"This morning . . . not over an hour ago . . . this renegade rabbi . . . I won't say his name . . . came to the outer Court and tried to destroy everything . . . everything!" The priest angrily spit out his words. "What will he next do to the Temple?"

The Temple was isolated from the city by huge courtyard walls, white as snow. The outer court was also known as the Court of the Gentiles, because that's where the bankers sat, changing money. They took our good Roman money and for a fixed discount exchanged it for temple coins. The bankers did a lively business, because every Isrealite over twenty years old had to pay a temple tax of an exact Hebrew half shekel. This was a required offering to Yahveh. Some bankers became as wealthy as Zio Ammonius. The sale of sacrificial animals also took place there. Emperor Tiberius ordered the daily sacrifice of a lamb and two bullocks for his own safety. Did our ruler want a blessing from Yahveh or was it a political gesture?

"Just how could this rabbi destroy everything?" Pilate asked. "You have guards. He was only one man."

"He and his followers watched our devoted worshippers put their corban into the treasury. When he saw a poor widow, he said,

She has put in more than all the others, for their offerings come from their abundance, but she gives more from her poverty and the little she has.

That's an insult to people like Nicodemus and Joseph! That rab . . . that . . . that man has no right to judge others like that!"

Pilate sighed, "Settle among yourselves who is the most generous. That's no concern of the emperor . . ." He turned away. Caiaphas' concern seemed a trivial matter. ". . .

But that's not all! He and his followers went through the court, throwing over the bankers' tables, flaying away with a scourge of rods. That . . .that man. . . cried out,

My father's house shall be one of prayer, not a den for thieves!

It was chaos. Coins rolled everywhere. Bankers fell on their knees to recover their lost money. Some pilgrims ran to scoop up the coins and denari, then fled. Sheep and doves were freed, too. Bleating lambs and flapping wings . . . it was terrible . . . just terrible." Aggrieved, the priest stood there wringing his hands and shaking his head.

"You have your own temple guards. Why didn't they arrest the rabbi?"

"How could they? It all happened so fast. He and his followers blended into the crowd. They had long robes and covered heads. People flooded the streets with their stolen coins." The priest continued, tearfully, "That . . . that man threatened to destroy the Temple and rebuild it in three days. He started today. Blasphemy! Shabbat healing! Now, he's defiled our Temple. Arrest him!" He fell into a chair, weeping in distress. "Can't you Romans understand anything?"

Pilate signaled Clodius to list all the charges against the Rabbi. Then he patted the priest's shoulder. "I know that the temple is sacred to you. Do you really believe with your long history as Yahveh's chosen people that this Rabbi from Nazareth can destroy your Temple in three days when it's still being restored?"

Even the priest saw the impossibility with the temple's great walls and rich appointments. Workmen were constantly adding to its grandeur.

Pilate's words calmed him, "Your Yahveh provided you with fine temples . . . those of Solomon and Zerubbabel, and now, this one . . . Herod's Temple. Such trouble disturbs me, too. However, the Rabbi will leave town . . . he always does. Go back to the temple and see that it's put in order again."

The priest was emphatic. "I warn you . . . if we find him, we'll arrest him. This time he's gone too far."

"The Rabbi has made his point," Pilate reminded him. "He knows he's in danger. No doubt, he'll move on to some other place . . . maybe Damascus." As he dismissed him, Pilate added, ". . . But remember, if you do find him, he's your problem . . . not mine."

Later, Tuum and I discussed the temple riot. Surely, the Rabbi committed a sin when he caused so much trouble. Some people stole money or lost their sacrificial animals in the melee. Maybe, the Rabbi wanted to make the templea house of prayer, but – as a result – didn't he caused others to sin?

"I'm very confused about sinfulness," I confessed to Tuum. "I thought sin was being bad, or defying the Ten Words, but it must be more than that."

"Why – Bibi –," she said in her direct and simple way, "sin is anything that separates us from Yahveh and our neighbor, too."

My sister – once my slave – was wisest of all.

That night Pilate awoke in great pain. He didn't allow Clodius to summon medical help until daylight, so everyone could get a night's rest. At the first hour, the Cohort doctor came. He prescribed light meals – which I supervised closely – baths, massages, an amulet of dried anemones and an offering of lizard's entrails to the god Ares. All this was standard care for anyone with liver problems. Also, an extra glass of wine was ordered with each meal. Pilate clutched his abdomen when the sharp pains hit. We decided to sleep in separate bedrooms because his groans and restlessness disturbed me. We were apart during the week.

The night before that fateful Passover Eve, my terrible nightmare returned. We were at the Black Palace at Machaeus. The prophet's head was brought in to young Salome – except the face was that of the Rabbi from Nazareth. I cried out until Tuum awakened me. She cradled my head in her lap and sponged my forehead with a cool damp cloth. My dark dream was an omen of a troubled day ahead.

Pilate slept fitfully, too. We were at an early breakfast together when Clodius announced that a Temple committee demanded to see Pilate. He assumed they wished to collect some religious robes. Their priestly clothing was stored and protected in the palace. Passover Eve was their Day of Preparation.

". . . At this hour?" Pilate snapped. "Show them into the great hall. They can pick up their robes there."

"They can't. Passover starts tomorrow. They would be unclean . . . unfit for their holy days if they came inside." Clodius added, "Anyway, they have an accusation to make."

Pilate grimaced with a sharp pain. "Now, what's their problem?"

"They have the Rabbi from Nazareth with them."

Tuum, who stood behind me, put her hand on my shoulder. Without turning around, I reached up and put my hand over hers. We scarcely breathed.

Pilate reached for his wine glass. It slipped from his hand and shattered on the floor. The wine splattered like drops of blood. That was another bad omen. Pilate leaned over and kissed the table – a sign to ward off any evil that might fall on him that day.

"Humph! How can that country Rabbi continually cause trouble? Take the tribunal bench and put it on the pavement out in front. They can see me there after I've changed my robe." Another pain hit him.

Tuum and I went to a window that overlooked the entrance. Along with the temple leaders, some angry moneychangers, traders and shepherds had joined the crowd. No doubt, they were still furious over the earlier temple riot. First, an enthusiastic crowd had welcomed the Rabbi to Jerusalem. Now they were turning against him because he claimed prayer was more important than money.

We saw Pilate sit down with two guards at attention. Clodius was nearby with his tablet and stylus to record the details. Pilate took time to carefully adjust the folds of his white robe, banded in purple, which signified that he was an Empire magistrate. He fully looked like a figure of Roman authority.

I studied the Rabbi's face. He watched Pilate – taking the measure of his Roman attitude and his authority. The Rabbi wore a homespun robe and dusty sandals. His shoulders slumped forward, as he sensed the hostility around him. His eyes were tired and sad. Perhaps he, too, had experienced a sleepless night.

Pilate cleared his throat, "What are the charges against this man?"

Immediately, there were shouts from all directions.

"This Galilean is an evil-doer who defiles our temple!"

"He calls himself the Messiah--the Son of Elohim!"

"He tells people to gouge out their eyes and cut off their hands!"

"He stirs up the people!"

"He's a lawbreaker!"

"He stays in Samaritis!"

"He eats with sinners!"

Someone shoved the Rabbi forward. He stumbled unsteadily.

Pilate was ill. His reports to Roma were due. He wanted to finish this case quickly. However, he had to be careful with provincial citizens. There were no formal written charges from the temple authorities, nor a jury as there would be in Roma. Old Tiberius would not be pleased if even a rabbi complained to him of mistreatment from Pilate.

Pilate restrained his anger. "You have your own laws. Judge him yourself!"

A minor priest called out, "Our laws won't permit us to put anyone to death. Only the Emperor has that power. You represent him."

Pilate weighed these words and then leaned toward the guard. "Bring him into the great hall. I wish to question this man alone."

Tuum and I dashed ahead to listen behind the golden screen. The Rabbi from Nazareth stood alertly before Pilate. They might have been two senators ready to discuss a petition in Roma.

Pilate considered the only question that mattered to him – one about power. Was this Rabbi planning an insurrection? Did he wish to be a king – like Herod, the Great?

Pilate asked directly, "Are you the King of the Jews?"

The Rabbi almost burst out laughing. "Did you hear me say this? Or did others say I made that claim?"

That was the Judaean way – answer a question with a question.

"Am I a Jew?" Pilate snapped, meaning Am I circumcised? He thought the practice was an unmanly and barbaric custom, quite unnecessary for intelligent Romans.

More words were exchanged about rulers and kingdoms.

Finally, the Rabbi exploded, "I believe that I was born for one thing in this world . . . to bear witness to the Truth. If you listen to me, you will know the Truth. And the Truth that I teach will make you . . . even you, a Roman . . . Free."

Free? I knew Pilate would never be free. He was forever obligated to the Emperor.

Pilate spit out, "What is Truth?" with a cynical snicker.

That's when Pilate made his mistake. He didn't wait for a reply. Why didn't he pursue what the Rabbi was teaching?

Then he could have released him. Or shipped him to Roma for a trial. But Pilate wanted a quick resolve. He remembered the Rabbi was a Galilean and under the jurisdiction of Herod Antipas.

He sent the Rabbi to Antipas, Tetrarch of Galilee, who was in Jerusalem for Passover. A wily one, he returned the Rabbi to Pilate with a note, "Behold your king! This is your territory, not mine. You decide what to do with him."

The soldiers had amused themselves and roughed up the Rabbi. They robed him in worn gold drapery and hung a heavy rope around his waist. His royal staff was a twisted branch, topped by a pottery image of Bacchus, god of wine. This was to ridicule his sacred meal, held the previous night.

The Rabbi was doomed. The Judaeans wanted justice for the Rabbi's offenses. Pilate wanted peace and harmony. And the Rabbi argued like a Galilean Socrates. He expected to change lives through his teachings and healing.

Three different backgrounds – Judaea, Roma and Galilee. Three languages – Hebrew, Latin, Aramaic. Three different goals – Justice, Order, and Truth. Truth and innocence should have won over all other concerns. However, Justice was portrayed blindfolded and unable to see Truth. And Justice, enforced by the state, was always subject to political realities. This time Justice would bow to the mob. Truth and innocence would be rejected. The Rabbi would die unless I interfered – something I had never dared to do before. Pilate's political office and decisions had always belonged to him alone.

"Tuum," I ordered, "run to Clodius. Have him tell my husband not to have anything to do with this business. The Rabbi from Nazareth is a holy man. I had a terrible dream about him last night. It still disturbs me. Go quickly!"

Tuum sped away. Shortly, I saw Clodius whisper something to Pilate. He rubbed his chin thoughtfully and looked toward my window.

Finally, Pilate called out, "You have a custom that I should release one man at Passover. Whom do you want me to release? Bar-Abbas, or . . . or . . ." He looked at the Rabbi, trying to recall his name. Clodius whispered to Pilate, who said aloud, ". . . Jesus who is called the Messiah?"

At this, the crowd erupted. "Bar-Abbas! Bar-Abbas!" They cheered their folk hero, who was a murderer, although he was considered a freedom-fighter, too.

Pilate, pale and troubled, frowned, "Then what shall I do with this truth-seeker?"

"Crucify him! Crucify him!" the mob shouted. Along with the money-changers, there were others like Greek shopkeepers, Syrian traders and

Egyptian weavers-still angry over the earlier riot when temple animals had escaped and smashed their stalls.

Tuum and I looked at each other. They sounded like spectators, yelling for blood, at Roma's big arena. Did the mob want one last entertainment before the holy days?

Pilate whispered to Clodius. Shortly, a young officer returned with a silver bowl. Sweet-scented pink rose petals floated in the water. Pilate swirled his hands a moment and called out, "I am innocent of this man's blood." He turned to Clodius, "Order Bar-Abbas released. Then scourge this man!"

Pilate leaned forward and grabbed his rib-cage as a sharp pain crossed his face. Grimly, he stalked into the palace. The crowd had outwitted him.

Was the Rabbi too proud to beg for mercy? Maybe, if the mob saw the Rabbi as a battered prisoner, it would satisfy their thirst for blood. Yes! Then Pilate could release him.

Both Tuum and I sobbed. We knew about scourging. The Roman method was to strip the prisoner, stretch him out on a frame and hold him down by leather thongs. First, he would be beaten with rods, then thirty-nine strokes with a short flag rum – a leather whip of tiny lead balls and sharpened bits of bone to sting and slash the flesh. It meant to weaken the prisoner, so any crucifixion would be a shortened, but horrible death. I had never seen an execution, but I knew that prolonged suffering could last for more than a day, before death occurred. Vultures would circle around the dying victim.

In the praetorium dungeon, the soldiers must have played the Basalinda game with the Rabbi. He returned, clothed in a dirty purple blanket with a crown of jujuba-tree thorns pushed down on his bleeding head. He held a bull-rush reed in his hand. The Roman soldiers had knelt and spit on him, laughing, "Hail, King of the Jews!"

When Pilate saw the Rabbi for the last time, he demanded, "Can't you speak? Don't you know that I have the power of life and death over you. I can release or crucify!"

The Rabbi struggled to speak through swollen lips. "You . . . have . . . no . . . power . . . over men unless . . . it's been . . . given . . . you . . . from above . . ."

"This man is innocent!" Pilate turned his back to reenter the palace.

The crowd shouted, "You are not Caesar's friend! Anyone who calls himself a KING   is against Caesar."

Pilate drew his right arm across his waist as another sharp pain hit him. A shrewd look crossed his face. Intelligent Romans didn't have kings . . . only provincial clans and fiefdoms wanted a monarch. He returned to his tribunal.

"Here is your KING!" said Pilate, mocking the crowd.

"We have no king but Caesar!" the mob shouted in unison.

A small smile crossed Pilate's face. If the crowd had manipulated him to crucify the Rabbi, he had caused them to acknowledge the Emperor as their supreme ruler. In his next dispatch to Roma, he could add that the Judaeans at Passover had shouted their allegiance to Tiberius. Old problems, like a census and hanging the Roman medallions, were over.

As a final gesture, Pilate arrogantly decreed that the Rabbi's heavy crossbeam be inscribed Jesus Nazarathaeus Rex Judaeorum – Jesus of Nazareth, the King of the Jews – in Aramaic, Latin and Greek. The temple authorities might protest. Cynical Pilate knew that Antipas would seethe, too, since he had schemed for the royal title.

"What I have written, I have written!" Pilate thundered. "That covers everyone . . . Antipas, the authorities, and the mob! No one escapes!" He went into the palace and slammed the bedroom door, glad to be done with the ugly scene.

Tuum and I went to the garden to read, but we couldn't concentrate. We were in a somber mood. Often, I looked away when I saw trash heaps or any ugliness. I knew that afternoon would be worse than anything I could imagine.

"If he is innocent," Tuum said, "Yahveh will save him. The prophet Isaiah wrote that those who depend on Adonai will gain new strength . . . they will soar on wings like eagles. That's what I believe."

I didn't know how to respond to Tuum's simple faith. Even if the Rabbi were a miracle worker, how could he escape crucifixion?

Our curiosity drew us to Golgotha hill. Or did we, also, have a human lust for blood, like the mob drawn to the macabre scene? We were surprised to see Cornelius there as the Centurion in charge. It had to be difficult, since he had always avoided that duty. Did Pilate order him to Golgotha?

Two other men also hung on crosses – a Parthian robber and a dim-witted young man who had stolen bread out of hunger. One look at the innocent Rabbi suffering there, and we had to leave. The three bloody crosses were even more gruesome than we expected.

The sky darkened, so we hurried even faster to avoid the storm. As we left, the Rabbi cried out, "Eloi – Eloi – why have you forsaken me?"

Tuum and I remembered. For the devout Jews, crucifixion meant that Yahveh had abandoned them entirely. We dashed into the palace just as the storm hit with high winds and lightening. Both Tuum and I were sad and silent for we were disturbed by the Rabbi's suffering figure. The Judaeans believed everyone should be treated fairly. Could there be any amends for such injustice?

After the storm, Tuum and I climbed the circular stone steps that led to the palace watchtower. To the north, we saw three crosses etched against the murky sky. The days of preaching, teaching and healing for the Rabbi were over. Death had ended his life.

Clodius reported that a wealthy Judaean had provided a tomb for the Rabbi's body. Pilate ordered the temple authorities to use their own guards to secure the place. He refused to see anyone else, as he was miserable and in great pain. The Cohort physician ordered a massage and sprinkled a foreign substance in a glass of wine to induce sleep.

Pilate remained in seclusion on Shabbat. Tuum and I read Praise-Songs in the garden, somber with the memory of the central cross and the Rabbi, poor and plain as a palace servant, suffering there.

Finally, Tuum said, "Bibi . . . remember that young man who was crucified because he had stolen some bread? Why don't we take a few loaves to the beggars at the pool of Siloam? Maybe that will help the heaviness in our hearts."

Did we break the laws of Shabbat by sharing our bread? I didn't want to ask that question. We slipped into our native dress and distributed two baskets of bread to grateful outstretched hands. It seemed a small way to relieve innocent suffering.

On the first day of the week, Tuum suggested that we feed the peacocks in the garden. She brought her flute along to ease my nerves. My night had been restless. Pilate – still ill – was sleeping late. As Clodius didn't want to disturb Pilate, he came to me instead.

"There is a report," Clodius frowned, "that the stone on the Rabbi's tomb has been moved. Should his Excellency be alerted? Perhaps the Zealots or the Herodians want to cause trouble during Passover."

I weighed his words. "No," I answered, "the crucifixions are over. The tomb is watched by the temple guards. Pilate is done with it all. Leave him alone." I waved Clodius away.

Lazily, I stretched out on some rose damask cushions and stroked a small cat, named Sheba. Tuum played her flute, ever so sweetly. I half-closed my eyes and felt I was in paradise, amid the sparkling fountains and scented lilies of the palace garden.

Although I tried, I knew I would never forget the Rabbi's trial and crucifixion. He died, trying to help people.

We left after Passover and returned to Caesarea. Pilate improved with the soft breezes from the Great Sea and the familiar surroundings in the Caesarea palace. His spies reported that some followers claimed that the Rabbi from Nazareth appeared to them at various times. An annual Pentecost celebration had been particularly spirited. Many believed that people had imbibed too heavily that day. Pilate drummed his fingers on his desk, thinking over everything.

"Forget it!" he said. "I'm done with the Rabbi from Nazareth."

Chapter XXIII

P ilate sent his report about the three crucifixions to Roma. There was no censure. Evidently, the Emperor's staff didn't attach any importance to the event. Nor did the temple authorities bring another lawsuit to Pilate that year. Rumors made them wary of creating a martyr. Pilate dismissed the trial and aftermath, especially the claim about an empty tomb. He ignored it all, governing as efficiently as ever.

Life was not so easy for me. My nightmare over the beheaded John the Baptist was now mingled with the suffering Rabbi, hanging on a cross. He had committed no political crime that justified his death. Why should anyone be persecuted for religious belief? I was haunted by the agony of three crosses, in silhouette against the sky.

Tuum and I meditated on scripture and comforted each other. We quietly discussed the Jerusalem experience with others at our weekly prayer meetings. Cornelius seemed especially reflective. He would shake his head over the crucifixion and repeat in a firm voice, "Truly, the Rabbi was the son of Elohim."

We returned to Jerusalem for the next Passover. Things were different. Some people were collecting memories and sayings of the Rabbi from Nazareth. They wanted my eyewitness account of the trial before Pilate. I only mentioned my warning to Pilate. I told them to ask Cornelius and the others about the event. I didn't want Pilate to face any more problems over the Rabbi.

Two spies reported that the Rabbi's mother went north to Ephesus with one of his disciples. Followers of the beheaded John the Baptist waited for his resurrection as the Messiah somewhere in Phrygia. These religious leaders were outside of Judaea and of no concern to Pilate.

One-night Pilate and I discussed famous people and how they were chosen by historians and scholars.

"A famous personage must leave behind some writings. Think of the great speeches and letters of Cicero," said Pilate. "There was a real intellect. He will be read a thousand years from now."

"He met a martyr's death. He lost his head and his hands, too." I shuddered.

"True. Then there's the two Greeks, Socrates and his pupil Plato."

"Socrates drank a cup of hemlock to avoid being killed. Plato wore himself out writing great masterpieces. Not easy ways to die." I reflected a moment. "I think the Rabbi from Nazareth will be remembered for a long time."

"Not possible!" Pilate argued. "He left no writings, no great orations. Even his stories were too simple . . . taken from nature. Not much of an intellect."

"His followers have collected some of his sayings."

Pilate leaned forward. "I'll guarantee, he'll be forgotten. What was he? A self-appointed messiah. How many have we had in history? No one understood what the Rabbi meant when he said kingdom. Earthly? Heavenly?" Pilate cleared his throat. "Sell all your property? Give money to the poor? Follow me? Where? He confused everyone. He's dead."

"Some believe that he appeared again." Pilate would scoff if I mentioned the mystical belief that Moses, Enoch, Elijah, and Isaiah all ascended into heaven and added the Rabbi.

"Procula, be sensible! The Rabbi was a moralist . . . an idealist. No one listens to a moralist for very long. Morality is the last thing that people want to hear. Society listens to powerful practical men . . . like the Emperor. Good men . . . even well-meaning ones like the Rabbi from Nazareth . . . are ignored."

Pilate was sure he was right. I was silent.

Vergil wrote in the AEneid VI –*quisque suos patimur manes.* We each suffer our own destinies.

Things were going well – maybe too well. We looked forward to a special celebration of Pilate's tenth anniversary as Prefect. Perhaps old Tiberiius would grant him an even higher status.

As I slept, curled around Pilate's warm body, I had a disturbing dream. I stood by the Appian Way near Roma. A great crowd of people surrounded me and were shouting with their fists raised in the air. "Death . . . death to the murderers," they cried. As I edged closer, I saw several prisoners stumbling under their heavy beams, on the way to crucifixion. As one looked up, his face was bloodied. I screamed. The prisoner was Pilate.

I awakened as Pilate gently shook me.

"Wake up. Procula . . . wake up." He rubbed my back and soothed my forehead. "Did you dream of the banquet at Machaerus?"

I lied, "Yes."

My restless dreams both amused and irritated him. That night, he chided me. "That was years ago. Go to sleep." He turned over and was snoring in a few minutes.

I was not so sure. I stayed awake that night, apprehensive about the future.

Two spies reported that Samaritan forces were gathering at Mt. Gerizim to recover golden relics that Moses had buried there. Pilate acted swiftly and too rashly. He didn't believe that any treasure would be found.

"Moses lived fifteen hundred years ago, if he lived at all," Pilate shrugged with skepticism. He never believed the accuracy of any history, but Roman. "I doubt if any golden artifacts ever existed . . . maybe a couple of golden cups and a brass lamp or two." After a moment of silence, he said, "If so, things were looted a long time ago."

He and a Captain studied the territorial map.

"It's possible that a Galilean force from Antipas' army might join the Samaritans at Mount Gerizim. They could march south . . ." the Captain traced the route. ". . . and be joined by Perean forces from the east. Then, Jerusalem would be vulnerable from both directions."

Pilate stroked his chin thoughtfully. "Unfortunately, our Roman roads can be used by enemy forces as well as friends." What he didn't say was that with a victory, Herod Antipas could reclaim his father's Judaean territory and regain the Herodian crown.

Over twenty years of peace had marked Tiberius' rule, the longest record in Roman history. Didn't the Emperor give Pilate a mandate to keep the peace? Pilate intended to end any rebellion before it began. He assembled his troops to march at night. He was confident and told me not to worry.

"If the Samaritans really have found Moses' treasure, I'll bring you a golden cup," Pilate promised. "Here . . . kiss my Mars ring as a token of victory."

My lips brushed the incised stone, but my heart wasn't in it. I didn't believe in superstitions any longer. I knew I would only pray to Yahveh for an end to bloodshed and for Pilate's safety – as selfish as that was. I no longer prayed for any Roman victory. Did war ever guarantee peace? Not in Roman history. Conquered people were always restless for a new leader to lead a new rebellion.

Uneasy, I waited for news. A courier arrived, breathless. "Roma is victorious! Pontius Pilate was brilliant and caught the Samaritans by surprise!"

The battle at Mt. Gerizim was short. The Samaritan leaders were crucified without a trial. Pilate returned home and sent word to Roma. Unfortunately, the defeated Samaritans appealed more quickly to

Vitellius, governor of Syria, who ranked above Pilate and enjoyed using his higher authority. Vitellius had never liked Pilate. His real interest was in his olive groves and a life of ease. When he heard the Samaritans' complaint, Vitellus ordered Pilate back to Roma on false charges of extortion and cruelty. At the news, Pilate collapsed. His hair turned white and his liver trouble worsened. Emperor Tiberius could be vindictive. He might order Pilate dragged through the streets and, ultimately, be crucified. Since Zio Ammonius was dead, there was no influential help anywhere.

"What did I do wrong?" Pilate asked me. "The Emperor wanted peace and order. I kept that. I finished the aqueduct. I never felt right about that Rabbi's death, but there were no riots in Jerusalem. I kept trade moving, so wheat reached Roma . . . no bread riots there, either. Taxes were collected and sent to Roma." He repeated, "What did I do wrong?"

I cradled his head in my arms and I felt his wet tears. "Nothing, my Eros. You tried your best to serve the Emperor." That was Pilate's problem. He had bowed to an earthly authority – to his sense of duty. Instead, his conscience should have answered to Yahveh.

Pilate completed his reports. We packed our personal possessions. I left the lovely marble inlaid table and brass urns. They belonged in a palace. We sent our boxes overland. Tuum insisted on coming with us, although a quarry owner wanted her to supervise his household.

Cornelius arranged a farewell military ceremony at the pier, giving Pilate honor and respect. Both had tears in their eyes as they gave final salutes.

Chapter XXIV

I insisted on sailing to Roma. I thought the sea air might strengthen Pilate for his ordeal ahead. Our first port was Joppa – a much older city than Caesarea, and important in overland trade. We stayed for two days, then sailed here to Alexandria, docking yesterday in early morning. Lucius met us with a carriage and brought us immediately to his large home, overlooking the sea. We had a quiet elegant dinner. Pilate retired early so that Lucius and I could discuss my financial affairs. Tuum and I shared a suite which overlooked the harbor. The sunset was brilliant – like a red and gold silk scarf trailing across the sky.

After midnight, the nightmare about the banquet and John the Baptist' bloodied head ended my rest. That is why I stayed awake, thinking about my life and our Judaean experience. The decade of service to Tiberius and the Empire is over. I pray the Rabbi's prayer daily, save us from the time of trial –and trials – which lie ahead.

Also, I pray for forgiveness of my many sins that I have willingly or unwittingly committed. I think of slapping Tuum, resentment of Zio Ammonius, my ridicule of Zia Terentia, hatred for Octavianus, my envy – yes, envy – for Iris' position as wife of the first-born son. If I really love Yahveh, why can't I love others more? I wish – even more – that I could atone for my sins – face to face – like the Judaeans during their days of Atonement. I am contrite, but that doesn't seem enough.

In the three years since the Rabbi's death, some Gentile followers have adopted Baptism as a sign of devotion to Yahveh and assurance that they belong to him. Tuum was baptized in the Jordan river a year ago. She ended her resentment over bitter childhood memories of abandonment and beatings. Now she radiates an inner joy because she says she belongs to Yahveh and can love others as the Rabbi from Nazareth taught. I want to be baptized, too, when we get to Roma. We hear his followers there are being persecuted. Will I be brave? I know Tuum will be.

It's a surprise to hear Lucius returning from his early morning walk. It's still quiet. I'm afraid that he brings the sad news of an earlier sailing time tomorrow. It will be so hard to say Good-bye to Lucius. I go into the atrium. Pilate holds his head in his hands. Tuum gently massages his shoulders.

As he strides in, Lucius abruptly announces, "Emperor Tiberius is dead!"

There's stunned silence. Pilate asks, "Are you sure?"

Lucius continues, "The Emperor was on his way to Roma. When he stopped at Lucullus' villa in Misenum, he fainted and died." Lucius hesitates. "Many rumors suggest that the couriers of Gaius really smothered Tiberius with a pillow . . . to assure that he was dead. Anyway, the Senate has quickly ratified Gaius Caligula as the new Emperor."

Tuum and I look at each other. Together, we circle our faces and wipe our palms across our mouth. Tomorrow will be a good day. Clodius will take our trunks to the ship in the morning. Pilate, Tuum and I will follow later on donkey cart. When it reaches a busy street, an axle – or it could be a wheel – will break. We will climb out and wait for the driver to find another cart. Until then, we three will wander along the shops, down an alley or two, and linger in a Syrian rug seller's shop. He will take us to a back room to show us even finer rugs. Time will pass. Later in the morning, three AEgyptians will emerge. Two of them will be women in native dress with facial veils. The man will wear a coarse-linen robe with a peasant head cloth and band. His face will be very brown, darkened with tannin.

Tuum and I know that when the ship leaves Alexandria, we won't be sailing. With Lucius' help, we will remain – unknown – in AEgyptus forever. However, southeast in Naukratis, customers will find a shop on a side street that sells quality linens and small rugs. It will be owned by two sisters.

Remember my destiny. I am Procula – far, distant, remote.

* * *

EPILOGUE – THREE YEARS LATER

Cornelius, Centurion of the elite Palace Guard, approached the office of General Marcellus with both wariness and curiosity. As a strict Centurion, he could not remember any infraction – even a minor one – in his unit. It was known for its daily drills, polished equipment and tight discipline. Cornelius was proud that his soldiers didn't get drunk or taunt the local Judaeans. After twenty years in the Roman army, he was close to retirement. His wife Esther wanted to live in the Greek Isles. Nothing must interfere with their plans.

Cornelius entered the office, noting a new marble bust of Emperor Gaius on a corner pedestal. Each year the Caesarea post received another carved image of the empire's ruler. Under their breath, the guards snickered that someday a room would be needed to hold all of them. An Imperial flag almost covered one wall. The General knew how to flatter the Emperor.

When Governor Vitellius of Syria ordered Pilate to stand trial in Rome, he quickly appointed General Marcellus as a temporary ruler until Emperor Tiberius could name a new Prefect. Then Tiberius was murdered. So far, his successor, Gaius, had failed to act. Gaius was building a splendid palace in Roma – the largest in the empire. Possibly, he had forgotten the Judaean appointment.

Cornelius gave a sharp salute which the General acknowledged.

"At ease," the General murmured and pointed to a chair.

The General was a large man, clipped in speech and obviously irritated with an order he held in his hand. He waved the document toward Cornelius.

"As you know, Pontius Pilate . . . my predecessor . . . disappeared three years ago on his way to Roma. It was assumed that his party went down with the ship, The Athenian Odyssey, which was lost in a storm."

"Yes, they drowned."

"Some rumors persist. One . . . that he never left Alexandria, but moved southward." Marcellus grimaced. "Another says he hides in the Alpes mountains . . . or . . . that he lives incognito in Belgico."

"How so? The ship sank. All were lost."

"Not everyone. After more than a week, two sailors floated ashore, clinging to a ship's rib. They claimed there were no travelers on board. Nor does the dockmaster have any passenger record."

"Clodius was sure . . ."

The General cleared his throat. "Clodius put Pilate's luggage on board. When the trio didn't arrive, he returned to Lucius' house . . . where they had stayed overnight . . . to hurry them along. Pilate and the two women had already left. By the time Clodius went back to the dock, the Odyssey had sailed. Clodius was shaken by his mistake in Alexandria."

Cornelius remembered that when Pilate vanished, Clodius was held responsible. Pilate's former aide was now a cook in a field unit.

"Where do I fit in?" Cornelius asked.

Marcellus continued, "You knew Pilate . . . and his wife . . . as well as any Centurion. I'm sending you to Alexandria to check out the rumor that Pilate is still in AEgyptus with his wife and her friend."

Cornelius thought of Esther and the children. "For how long?"

"Six weeks. Take one of your own soldiers as an assistant. Your papers and funds are in this packet. You will lodge in the Alexandria fortress, unless you go elsewhere." The General paused. "Another thing . . . you may dress as a native, if that is helpful." He added with a cynical laugh, "However, it hasn't helped any of our spies currently there. Pilate's coins never bore his profile. We have no drawing of him or his wife. Only you can recognize them. That is most important."

Cornelius took a deep breath. "I'm not a spy. I hardly know where to begin."

"Pilate's party stayed in the house of Lucius, who is a well-respected financial advisor in the city . . . and a man of property. At one time, he had some connection with Pilate's wife. You might start there."

Cornelius remembered how warmly Procula spoke of Lucius who was her uncle's steward when she was a child in Roma.

"– And if I find them?"

"Return here. AEgyptus is not in my jurisdiction." General Marcellus was quiet. "I've gone over the decade of Pilate's records. Maybe a few questionable expenditures, but most are in order. I think the search is a foolish mission. I don't know why Vitellius hated Pilate, but I must follow his orders." He sighed, "Who knows what will happen in these times?"

The General didn't need to explain. Cornelius knew all the stories about Emperor Gaius. He was short in statue and called Caligula or Little Boot because, as a boy, he imitated the soldiers who wore a half boot (caliga). At first, Gaius was generous, friendly, promised low taxes and civic celebrations. However, he had become heady with power, boasting that I have the right to do anything to anybody. So in Roma no man's wife was safe from Caligula's sexual appetite. Everyone, including Vitellius and Marcellus, lived in fear of the ruler's wrath.

Cornelius saluted the General. "Sir, I will do my best to find the three."
"I know you will. May the gods. . . that is, the spirit of the Emperor . . . go with you," the General added with a sigh. He saluted, too, and filed the search order away.

Apprehensive, Cornelius left. If he found Procula – and the other two – how could he betray them?

In Alexandria, it took a week before Fabius, his military aide, could arrange an appointment with Lucius. Obviously, Lucius didn't want to see him. As Cornelius sat in a garden loggia, he counted twelve lotus blossoms floating in a nearby pool. Impressed by the splendid garden, Cornelius grew more curious about the wealthy financier.

Finally, Lucius approached him, a regal figure in a bronze silken caftan. His hair was wooly white. His forehead bore the deep creases of heavy responsibilities. A ruby ring sparkled on one hand. A cameo with a Roman girl's profile was on the other. Gold chains hung around his neck. Two servants followed him with trays of dried fruit, cups of sweet wine and snowy towels.

Cornelius stood to offer a handshake. Lucius ignored him and took a chair. He motioned for Cornelius to sit down. The black man's face was impassive.

Lucius frowned. "So . . . you want to question me? I know nothing," he said, slowly sipping his wine. "I bid dear Procula, Tuum and Pilate good-bye that morning." He drew a linen piece from his sleeve and dabbed at his eyes. "So sad. They were lost at sea."

Did Lucius fake his emotion? Cornelius asked, "Tell me . . . who drove them to the pier that morning?"

Lucius shrugged, draping his caftan across his knees. "I don't know. My houseboy hailed some carrier along the street."

"Perhaps, I could question your slave."

Lucius glared at him. "There are no slaves in my household! I employ servants . . . often students who come to Alexandria to study and use the great library. That one went back to Thracia. Go, question him there!" Lucius turned away and wiped his lips with his towel.

Cornelius knew the useless interview was over. He had gained nothing. He, too, sipped wine and lifted the towel to his lips. His hand stopped as he glanced at the towel's blue border. The pattern looked so familiar. Where had he seen it? Of course! In the Caesarea palace! Procula was proud of her linens, marked with that distinctive pattern. Carefully, Cornelius spread the towel across his knees and neatly refolded it. His face didn't reveal any excitement.

In a genial tone, Cornelius replied, "It's generally accepted that they drowned . . . so tragic for everyone. I was merely sent from Caesarea to complete the report."

Lucius relaxed. "It's best to accept what happened. Pilate was your commander. Did you know Procula, too?"

"Yes. At times, she and Tuum came to Shabbat eve supper. Esther, my wife, is a Judaean. She was helpful to Procula in Caesarea." Slowly, Cornelius ate a dried apricot. He picked up the towel. ". . . Such fine quality. I would like to take some towels back to my wife. Where can I purchase these?"

Lucius paused. "Don't spend time in the markets." He motioned to the younger servant. "Bring a dozen new towels . . . a gift for our guest."

Shortly, the servant brought a package to Lucius. "There are no new towels left with a blue border. These have a green design. They arrived yesterday from Naukratis . . ."

Lucius interrupted. "I hope your wife will accept this present," he said curtly.

"Of course." Cornelius rose as he took the package. "I also thank you for your gracious hospitality. May peace always be in your household."

"Peace," Lucius mumbled and walked into his mansion.

Cornelius smiled. Lucius was worried that he heard Naukratis. His interview had been successful. He knew where he would find Pilate, Procula and Tuum – in a town of Greek traders and women merchants, southeast of Alexandria.

Alone, Cornelius – dressed in a native robe and headscarf – showed a towel to a Naukratis vendor. The merchant quickly identified it as "the finest quality, made by the House of the Two Sisters." For a coin, the vendor's son led Cornelius to a three-story building with high windows. The clatter of looms floated from an upper floor.

A terra cotta plaque – a bas-relief with two women in profile – marked the entrance. Nearby, two young boys tossed small stones onto pavement squares to accumulate points in a child's game.

PROCULA | Marion H. Youngquist

Cornelius stepped inside. Tuum and Procula were arranging shelves of linens on the opposite wall. As the entrance bell tinkled, Tuum turned around. She gasped, "Oh!" Her hand covered her mouth.

"Tuum?" Cornelius smiled. "Procula?"

Procula's back stiffened. Slowly, she turned around. "No one by that name is here. My sister is called Ruth. I am Miriamne. We own this linen business together. Are you interested in some fine cloth?"

Cornelius noted a gray streak at Procula's temple. Her hair was held sleek and smooth with large combs. Both women accentuated their eyes with dark lines and wore red lip rouge in the AEgyptian manner. Even their fingernails were painted. With their simple linen tunics, they wore wide silver and amber necklaces. Procula, well-tanned, could easily pass for a native.

"I'm interested in you . . . and Tuum . . . and Pilate. How are you doing?"

"Fine!" snapped Tuum, "until you came along!"

Procula held up a hand. "Wait! Are you here to arrest us? It won't help you. We have only to say the word, and you'll be jailed for alleged robbery. By the time you establish your identity as a Centurion, we'll be gone."

Cornelius shook his head. "I was ordered only to find out if you were still alive. I can't arrest you. We shared meals together, prayed together . . . and argued together." He paused, "So, you're not in danger . . . for now. How is Pilate?"

Tuum laughed, "There's no one here by that name either.

However, Socrates is in the back room with his books."

Procula protested, "Don't listen to her! Pilate is now called Nicolaus. People think he was born in Roma of Greek parents. Mainly, he keeps to himself. He handles our records and occasionally writes a contract for a neighbor."

Tuum raised her eyebrows. ". . . And reads. He is a thinker, now, just like the real Socrates."

The two young boys, playing outside, burst into the room.

"He didn't play fair!" the smallest yelled, pointing a dusty finger at his brother.

Tuum reached out her arms to him. "Come to Zia Ruth," she said, stroking his hair.

The older boy shrugged, "I let you win most of the time!

Forget the game!"

Procula spoke sharply. "Manners, my sons! We have a guest." She drew the oldest to her. "This is Joseph, and his brother is Benjamin. They came to live with us when their mother died. So, you see, I am no longer Procula. I am
Miriamne , their mother!"

"And I am an aunt!" Tuum added.

"Take our guest to your father," Procula said, turning Joseph toward Pilate's door. She smiled at Cornelius. "You're in for a surprise."

Cornelius was stunned by Pilate's appearance. Formerly, Pilate had stood ramrod straight with an almost arrogant stance. Now he was stooped and flabby with a bulging waistline and balding head. Instead of a smooth-shaven Roman face, he had grown a long white beard. A wig, like the AEgyptians wore, was on a corner stand. No one would recognize him as the former Roman Prefect of Judaea.

"Your Excellency . . . ." Cornelius began.

Pilate stopped him. "No title, please. I'm Nicolaus, the Greek, who married a Judaean with a sister. My two sons will keep my memory alive when I die. My life is like the Judaeans and AEgyptians. I long for freedom from the Romans!"

"You are well?"

"Yes. When I was recalled to Roma, my faith in the emperor and the army ended. I had always assumed that the emperor cared about me. When the emperor was ready to crucify me on false charges, my confidence vanished. Fear took over. I was without hope. All my victories and success became meaningless." Pilate slowly stroked his beard. "Remember that Rabbi from Nazareth who was crucified several years ago?"

Cornelius nodded. "Too well," pained by the memory.

"I made a mistake that Friday." Pilate continued. "I should have sentenced the Rabbi to prison in Caesarea. After three months, I could have released him with an order that he never enter Judaea again. He could have gone back to Galilee and joined his fishing friends on the Sea of Galilee. Tempers would have cooled in Jerusalem and the Temple authorities would have forgotten him." He reflected a moment. "I was blind and fearful of the crowd. I admit I was weak."

"So you still think about the Rabbi's crucifixion?"

"In our private conversation, the Rabbi challenged me . . . If you listen to me, you will know the Truth, and the Truth will make you free. Then I taunted him, What is Truth? So . . . now that is my passion. I search for TRUTH. Socrates, Plato, Varro . . . I read them all. I contemplate the Rabbi's sayings about forgiveness. I wonder . . . will I, too, be forgiven? Will I ever be free? Sometimes, I think the Rabbi pursues me now."

"Many who were there now seek forgiveness." Cornelius added softly, "He never gave up on anyone."

"Even when I let the crowd have its way, I don't think the Rabbi hated me. I think he felt a deep sadness. Procula reads Praise-Songs to me . . . *"A broken and a contrite heart, O Lord, you will not despise"* . . . It's a little solace and mercy for all my wrong decisions made for the right reasons!" Pilate reflected, "My life? Study. Think. And keep Procula's records!"

Procula entered, reached down and embraced Pilate. "We pay Pilate a salary, too," she laughed, ". . . along with all the hated Roman taxes!"

"So business is good?"

". . . And growing!" Pilate replied. "Her weavers work on the third floor. She pays them well, so they are loyal. Most of her workers are men!"

"It's not unusual for women to own businesses in Naukratis." Procula added proudly, "Our monthly shipments go to a warehouse in Alexandria. Lucius has a manager who sends them on to Roma. Eastern caravans also buy our linens."

Pilate stroked her hand affectionately. "My Procula . . . and Tuum . . . have turned out to be astute businesswomen like others in this town," he laughed, "while I pursue Truth . . . a more elusive mistress!"

In the outer room, Procula delayed Cornelius, ". . . And our Praise group in Caesarea . . . what has happened to it?"

"We have heated discussions over the Rabbi from Nazareth. Some believe he was the greatest teacher that ever lived. Others say he was a great miracle worker . . . or the promised Messiah. Others call him a prophet . . . but I think he was the son of Yahveh."

Thoughtfully, Procula nodded. "How I wished I had interfered and begged Pilate to leave the Rabbi alone. He could have dismissed the case."

"When the Rabbi cried out on the cross, Forgive them for they know not what they do, I felt he spoke directly to me."

". . . To all of us. The Rabbi died because of good . . . but weak . . . people like us. Remember how he called Yahveh, his Father?   Truly, he lived like a loving son. Perhaps someday his stories and prayers will be collected to share with others."

Cornelius didn't reveal to anyone that Procula, Tuum and Pilate were alive. He only wanted General Marcellus to hear his report. His nights were restless, trying to reconcile duty versus betrayal. He had found the three, but under assumed names. He stared at the ceiling, night after night. His eyes ached from loss of sleep. What to do?

Slowly he walked down the corridor to meet General Marcellus. His feet were heavy as lead on the stone floor. With a grave face, he saluted the General.

Again, the General pointed to a chair. "At ease. So you were gone . . . how many . . . five weeks?"

Cornelius tried to speak. Words wouldn't come. He cleared his throat.

The General held up his hand. ". . . No need to give me any report. I feel I owe you an apology. Since I sent you away, the whole situation has completely changed in your absence."

"What do you mean?"

"First, Emperor Gaius has appointed me Prefect of Judaea, Samaria and Idumaea."

"Congratulations!"

"I'm not sure that I want it, but I have my orders. It's dangerous to refuse, and it's almost as dangerous to be Prefect," he grimaced. "However, the Emperor has recalled Governor Vitellius to Roma to be tried on charges of corruption. Actually, the Emperor is jealous of the Governor.

It may mean torture and death for Vitellius."

". . . Like Pontius Pilate," Cornelius murmured.

"Exactly! But, without Vitellius, there's no case against Pilate." General Marcellus tapped his table. "These are difficult times. The Emperor has appointed Herod Agrippa the First as King of Syria. He's a grandson of Herod the Great. Now he rules over his relatives. Not good. Our spies report that Antipas will be deposed and sent to Lyons in Gaul, along with Herodias." The General shook his head. "Even worse . . . Emperor Gaius in Roma has declared himself a god. His statue must be in every temple. The Judaeans compromised with other emperors by offering prayers for them. Prayers aren't enough for Gaius. Surely, protest riots will erupt over his statue."

"Already," Marcellus continued, "the Christiani , a strange sect that follows a dead prophet Chrestus, has refused to worship Gaius. They were torn apart by wild lions in a bloody spectacle. People in Roma were horrified and sickened by such persecution."

Cornelius remembered too well how the Rabbi from Nazareth – the Chrestus – died on a Golgotha cross. Was there never any end to persecution and death?

The General rose. "Well, that's enough of my problems. Your trip must have been a strain. You look tired. Take a few days and get some rest. Anyway, thanks for your effort." His hand touched his brow.

Cornelius returned his salute and left.

Roma *locuta, causa finita* – Roma has spoken, the case is ended.

CONCLUSION

Only legends describe the fate of Procula and Pilate. The truth is unknown.

Pilate's wife, unnamed in Matthew's gospel, is called Claudia (Claudii clan) Procula in apocryphal sources. She is honored by both the Coptic and Greek Orthodox churches. She is remembered on October 27th.

Pilate is canonized in the Coptic church, being honored each June 25th. A prayer, written on parchment in Coptic, is attributed to him and preserved in the Ashmolean Museum in Oxford, England.

The End

NOTES

Antipas – son of King Herod the Great and Malthrace, a Samaritan. At Herod's death, he inherited Galilee and Peraea, being named a Tetrarch. He was considered sly and ambitious, but not as able as his father. His first wife was a daughter of an Arabian king. Then he eloped with his niece Herodias (daughter of his half-brother Aristobulus). She was also wife of his half-brother, Philip. This defiled Jewish law and incurred the wrath of John the Baptist.

Herodias persuaded him to go to Rome and demand to be made King. Instead, he had to confess that he had stored armor for 70,000 soldiers, and conspired with Sejanus and Artabanus, king of Parthia, against the imperial government. He was banished to Lyons in Gaul (France) and later died in Spain.

His brother was ARCHAELAUS, who was exiled earlier to Vienna in 6 C.E. Antipas was jealous of his nephew (and also brother of Herodias) Herod Agrippa the first, who was given Antipas' territory.

Archaelaus – Herod the Great's will provided that Archaelaus be made King, but fifty Jews sailed to Rome and urged that a Roman procurator be appointed. Instead, Caesar Augustus appointed him Ethnarch over half the territory
(Samaritis, Judaea, and Idumaea). However, his rule was so harsh (three thousand slain in the Temple, etc.) that he was banished in 6 C.E. to Vienna in Gaul.

Caiaphas – A high priest during Jesus life and throughout Tiberius' reign, 14 C.E.-38 C.E. He was the son-in-law of Annas, former high priest. He also exhibited great fury at the first efforts of the Apostles. He was deposed by procounsel Vitelllius after Tiberius' death.

Herodias – She was daughter of Aristobulus, son of Herod the Great. He and his mother, Mariamne, (and other family members) were executed by Herod who feared a plot to depose him. Her first husband was her step-uncle Philip I, half-brother to Antipas. (Philip's mother was also a Mariamne, the Boethusian – not the wife of the same name slain by Herod the Great). Herodias eloped with Antipas, although both were married at the time. Her daughter Salome (so-called by Josephus) was from her marriage to Philip I. Herodias was banished with Antipas to Gaul. (See Antipas above.)

Herod the Great – A ruler, descended from Idumeans (of Esau's line) who entered Palestine about 130 B.C.E. (The Herod clan adopted the rite of circumcision and the Jewish religion. Faithful Jews considered them half-Jews). Herod's army sided with the Romans. When Herod captured Jerusalem, he was named King by the Roman Senate. He removed the old temple and hired ten thousand skilled workmen to teach stone cutting to the priests. The great "white temple" was adorned with a pinnacle of gold. Work continued for decades until six years before it was destroyed by the Romans in 70 C.E. His new cities and palaces copied Greek buildings. He promoted a Roman lifestyle.

Herod was a heathen in practice, and a monster in character. He had ten wives and fourteen children. Always fearful of being deposed, he murdered members of his family. He died in 4 B.C.E. at age sixty-nine, hated by his people. It was said that "he stole to the throne like a fox, ruled like a tiger, and died like a dog."

Judas – Probably a Zealot who lived during Archaelaus rule in Judaea (4 B.C.E.- 6 C.E.) Not the Judas Iscariot of Jesus' ministry.

Machaerus – A centuries-old protection against Arab invaders, the Black Fortress was rebuilt by Herod the Great. It was located east and some three thousand eight   hundred and sixty feet above the Dead Sea. According to Josephus, Roman historian, John the Baptist was imprisoned in the dungeon beneath an elaborate banquet hall.

Maecenas, Caius Cilnius – A Roman statesman and trusted advisor to Caesar Augustus.

Pharisees – Separatists who strictly observed the Law, especially laws relating to cleaness and uncleaness. Originally, they may have been Scribes. They had decisive influence in public affairs, and in acts of public worship. They accepted immortality, the existence of angels and spirits, and in Divine Providence. Some adopted special behavior such as Tumbling Pharisees who hung their heads to appear humble and often fell. After the Temple's destruction (70 C.E.) the Pharisees became teachers and leaders in the synagogues. There were some 6,000 Pharisees in Biblical times.

PROCULA | Marion H. Youngquist

Philip II – He ruled in northeastern Batanaea, Trachonitis and Auronitis. He married his niece Salome, the daughter of Herodias and Philip I (his half-brother). They had no children. He built a new city, Caesarca Philippi, and had a long rule of moderation. He was the first Jewish prince to use images on his coins. After his death, his territory was annexed to the province of Syria.

Pontius Pilate – A Roman Prefect, administrator of Judaea. Samaria and Idumea which was a second-class province, during the reign of Emperor Tiberius He was under the direction of Vitellius, Governor of Syria, and served for a decade (26 C.E.-36 C.E). Pilate made six major mistakes as Prefect 1. Placed the Emperor's standards on the Antonio Fortress in Jerusalem; 2. Used corban, Temple funds, to complete an aqueduct; 3. Placed golden shields with the names of pagan deities in the Jerusalem palace; 4. Attacked and killed Samaritans on Mt. Gerizim, sacred to them; 5. Killed Galileans, who wanted to make Temple sacrifices; and 6. Crucified a Galilean rabbi, Jesus of Nazareth.

Saduccees – Priestly aristocrats who acknowledged only the written Law as binding. They rejected tradition and further development of the law. They doubted immortality and enjoyed good things in life. With the high priests, they belonged to the conservative faction of the Sanhedrin.

Salome – The daughter of Herodias and her first husband Philip I. Her dance resulted the death of John the Baptist. She (and her mother Herodias) defied the cultural norm of a young girl's strict seclusion from the opposite sex. Her first marriage was to Philip II, a step-uncle whose mother was Cleopatra of Jerusalem (fifth wife of Herod the Great). There were no children from this marriage. Her second marriage was to her cousin, Aristobulus, King of Chalcis. They had three sons.

Sanhedrin – A council of seventy-one leading priests, scribes and prominent laymen in Jerusalem, who had final authority in religious matters. It had its own police force and meted out all sentences, except the death penalty. That task belonged to the Roman prefect /administrator.

Scribes – These were Biblical scholars (and teachers) – zealous keepers of the Law. Respect – even greater than for parents – was accorded them. Teaching and interpretation gave them great authority since every Israelite needed wise help and acquaintance with the Law. They could act as judges.

Yahveh – a Gentile term, probably contracted from Jehovah. To obey the Second Commandment, "You shall not take the Name of the Lord in vain," and to obey the prohibition against blasphemy in Lev. 24:16, the Jews do not use the Holy Name.

When Jehovah established his covenant with Abram, he said, "I am EL SHADDI, God Almighty." According to Jewish tradition, the Holy Name was pronounced once a year on the Day of Atonement when the high priest entered into the Holy of Holies sanctuary.

Often YHVH is written, but read aloud as Adonai. When
Gentiles are spoken to or spoken about, Elohim represents the Holy One in
his relation to the world. Such reverence is unknown in present culture
where God and Jesus Christ are part of slang usage.

* * *

PROCULA is the author's attempt to look at the events of the era in a new
way. It occurs at a time when Christianity was forming and still connected
to its Jewish heritage. Latin words and phrases are used to lend an authentic
note.

The author depended on Caesar and Christ by Will Durant, Simon and
Schuster, New York, 1944, for final historical accuracy.

RESOURCE MATERIAL

Atlas of the Bible, Joseph Gardner, Editor, The Reader's Digest Assn. Inc., Pleasantville, N.Y., 1981.

Caesar and Christ, Will Durant, Simon and Schuster, New York 1944.

Chronicle of the Roman Empire, Chris Scarre, Thames and Hudson, Ltd. London 1995.

Cassell's Latin dictionary, Latin-English and EnglishLatin, rev. by J.R.V. Marchant and Joseph F. Charles, Funk and Wagnalls, New York, 1958.

Desire of the Everlasting Hills, Thomas Cahill, Doubleday, New York, 1999.

Jesus and his times, The Readers Digest Association, Inc., Pleasantville, N.Y., 1987.

Pontius Pilate, Ann Wroe, Random House, New York 1999.

The People's Bible Encyclopedia, Charles Randall Barnes, Editor, The People's Publication Society, Chicago, 1924.

PROCULA | Marion H. Youngquist

GARY DRURY PUBLISHER | KENTUCKY

druryspublishing.com

www.ingramcontent.com/pod-product-compliance
Lightning Source LLC
Chambersburg PA
CBHW050348030726
47503CB00008B/2667